WOMEN LIE MEN LIE - PART 1

A. ROY MILLIGAN

D1518678

To my uncle Eddie Milligan and my cousin Darrell Earl. In my heart you'll always be remembered R.I.P.

ACKNOWLEDGMENTS

MUCH LOVE AND thanks to God for blessing me with this opportunity. Nothing is possible without him. Thanks to my homeboy, Randy Jackson, for being an inspiration to me during this endeavor.

Thanks to you Mom, for keeping this a secret, until it made it to book form, and I love you for that. Thanks for all your help over the years.

Thanks to Mike Fields a.k.a. GSXR Mike, you read so much of my work. Thanks for giving me your honest opinion. It's going down . . . .

I also want to give some shout-outs, first, to my sister, Crystal Milligan, a busy, hard working woman, I love you. Shout-out; to my cousin Marlen Foggan a.k.a. Cho, and the rest of my family. Love you all, no matter what!

Shout-out to my homeboy G from Detroit, (Told you I would).

Oh, and wait, I can't forget to thank the one and only woman that inspired me to write, Wahida Clark. I Love your work. Finally a big, huge thanks to my readers. Thanks for all your support, you all are the best! I APPRECIATE all the letters and emails you send, keep them coming. I'm nothing without you. I love hearing from you all.

CHAPTER 1

JC woke up to the sound of "chow!" It was 6:30 a.m.
When he got off his bunk. He was tired and he still had
sleep in his eyes.

"Merido, wake up," he said to the foreign guy on the bottom
bunk. "Chow time." JC opened his locker and reached for his
toothbrush and toothpaste. He walked all the way down the
hall to the bathroom as everyone else was leaving to go eat.
"Damn," he said, turning around to go back to his cell to get his
washcloth. He jogged back to his room, opened his locker and
grabbed it, then jogged back down to the bathroom. He walked
inside the quiet bathroom and started brushing his teeth and
washing his face. Thirty seconds later, A 6'7", 300-pound guy
walked in, followed by two other guys.

"Yeah, we found out, you get out today. What do you plan to do
about that $23 debt you owe from the poker table?"

"I'll just drop it in your account when I get out," JC replied.

2 A. ROY MILLIGAN

"Why should I believe that? I been doing time for eighteen years, you think I'm stupid or something?"

"Naw, naw, I'm serious. I can get it to you soon as I touch down, Big J."

"Fuck that! You gonna have to pay me before ya leave!"

JC tensed up and knew there was about to be some shit. The whole time JC was locked up, he had been winning in poker. That was his hustle because no one on the outs sent him money. He had got in so many arguments and fights while gambling. If the parole board had known about those conflicts, he would have ended up doing ten more years, but today his time was up. It was time to go back to the streets.

All three guys rushed him, the biggest one knocking him to the ground with one hard punch to the jaw. JC kicked and tried to swing back. He kicked one to the wall and pulled one down on the dirty-piss smelling floor with him, punching him in the mouth. But Big J stopped all of that real quick. He kicked him right on the side of his head with his steel-toed boot. After that they all started beating him stripping his prison uniform off him at the same time.

JC kept fighting and kicking but he could only swing for so long. Big J was holding him over the toilet, kneeing him in the ribs, while one of the guys was pulling down his pants, getting himself ready. He pulled some Vaseline out of his pocket, opened it up and dug his hand inside, putting a big glob around his dick and smearing some between JC's ass cheeks. He started rubbing against JC from behind trying to jam his penis in, but JC kept moving and wiggling. Big J kneed him right in the face and shouted out to stop moving. Ryan was halfway in, and you could hear JC start to squeal.

CHAPTER 2

Merido woke up realizing his bunky just got him up for breakfast. He had three days left before he went home himself. He had done five long years. He got up put on his shoes and then walked straight to the bathroom to piss before he went to breakfast. He was already late, so he wasn't going to bother to brush his teeth or anything. He pushed the bathroom door open and saw three guys on JC. "What the fuck?"

He started pulling them off and swinging on all of them until Big J punched him and caused him to fall to the floor, but he got right up and kept swinging until all three of them ran out of the bathroom.

"JC, you alright?!" he asked, helping him up. JC was in serious pain. He had Vaseline and blood all over. They had messed him up over $23. But in prison, $23 is like $350 in the outside world. Every dollar counts for at least ten when you're locked up. Merido got there just in time because a minute later they would have torn JC a new asshole. They had missed breakfast just for that purpose but only one succeeded.

JC walked back to his cell with Merido, limping. He had to clean himself up before a C/O caught him.

"What was that about?" Merido asked, mad as hell.

"Man, I owed them from a poker game."

"What the hell you are gambling for if you on your way home?!"

"This was like two weeks ago."

"That's still a violation. When you going home from prison man, as soon as you get that Parole six months before your out date, you supposed to stay sucka free, and keep to yourself. You should not have been fucking with nobody, you fucked that up." Merido was mad at JC because he knew better. "And on top of that you know you coulda asked me for anything. Man, good luck out there in the real world, because you acting real stupid right now."

JC couldn't say a word. He felt like a little sunflower seed. He had just got raped over $23 on his out day. He was listening to everything Merido was preaching about. He definitely had to straighten up and get his mind right before he went outside the gates or he would be right back. Before this incident he had his mind set on grabbing a sack of dope again when he got out, but having another man fucking him was a big flash in his life. He was now almost careless, not wanting to waste his time selling drugs, when he can just take people's money, especially from his so called friends that should have been looking out for him while he was locked up.

CHAPTER 3

About an hour later he was lying on his bunk when his cell door opened. "Jason Cakes, time to go." The guard helped him carry his things and walked him to the front so he could be booked out. He could see Rita right behind the glass waiting for him to come through the metal detector. She was smiling from ear to ear until she saw his face was bruised and swollen. She could tell he had been in a fight. They let him through the door, and he and Rita hugged and kissed. They hadn't seen each other in person for like a year. Rita was banned from seeing him until he got released.

"Hey boo, what happened?" she whispered.

"I'll tell you later in the car. Let's get out of here," he whispered back. Rita had stood by his side the whole time he was in. The only bad thing about that was she didn't have extra money to send him and when she did, it was only like $5. She had bills of her own to pay, and he understood that, so it wasn't a problem. They got in the car and JC couldn't stop smiling. He was out of the hell hole. Even though he left beat up and raped, he was just happy to finally be out.

"Where we going?" he asked.

"To my house to eat. I cooked for you."

That sounded good to JC, but he had more important stuff to do before he could even think about eating. He had to first see his parole officer. He wasn't trying to catch a violation for showing up late or something stupid like that. So, he let her know to first take him there. They sat in there for about two hours, then left and went to Rita's house.

"What's this Facebook stuff I've been hearing about and how does it work?" He asked, sitting on the computer chair.

"Oh, I'll teach you what to do on it. Boy, do you have a lot of catching up to do! But don't worry, I got you boo. Don't you want to eat some real food first?"

"Hell naw, I wanna learn this Facebook shit, I heard a lot about it. I heard people be on there grinding hard, with their music and whatever else they do."

"Oh yeah it's exclusive. You can do a lot of stuff on there."

"So, you gonna show me boo?"

"Right now, JC?"

"Yeah, please," he smiled.

Rita motioned over to sit on his lap while she set everything up on the computer. They sat there for hours as she explained to him how everything works. She even helped him set up his own page.

Hours later after they were done playing on the computer, they relaxed in Rita's queen size bed. They talked, fucked, and then went straight to sleep.

Later that night while Rita was sleeping, JC crept and went through her expensive purse, took $200 out of her wallet and stashed it in his jacket. He then laid right back in bed and went to sleep.

CHAPTER 4

7 *months later*

"I love you," Welma said as she pulled JC closer to her, opening her legs wider allowing him to go deeper inside her.

"I love you too, boo," JC lied straight to her face. He was breathing hard and his body was still jerking from the fluids he had just released inside of her. He was only 21 but he loved messing with older women. He knew how to make them happy, make them cum, and make them fall in love with him.

JC was a very sweet and handsome young man. He stood 5′11″ at 185 pounds with an eight pack. With clear caramel skin, he resembled the singer O in the face. He also had a quarter of Cherokee in him. His hair was down to his back and he kept it braided nice and neat. He received checks in the mail every two weeks totaling $600, plus he worked as a janitor at a bank. He had been working at a bank for three months now and was making $9.00 an hour, five days a week and five hours a day.

He only brought about $800 a month home from that job, but he was making it pretty well.

"What would you like to eat this morning, honey?"

"Whatever you cook baby, you the best in the kitchen," JC said.

Welma smiled and made her way to the kitchen. She was a lonely lady but very wealthy. She was 45 years old, her kids were all grown up and off at college. Her ex-husband was out of the picture, so all she did was work. She made plenty of cash working at a bank as a supervisor, plus she had $125,000 in the bank from her divorce. She owned her condo and she owned two vehicles, a gray BMW SUV and a navy-blue Lexus Sedan.

JC was loving his life with Welma, because he didn't have to pay for anything at all, plus he could drive her cars anytime he wanted. She also gave him $150 a week for an allowance. All he did with this money was put it in a big safe that he kept at her house. JC was trying to save up $300,000 to open a convenience store. He had done a lot of research on running that kind of business and was on a mission. He already knew a guy who ran two convenience stores who told him he would sell him one when JC had the money.

CHAPTER 5

Welma made JC hash browns, eggs and toast before leaving for work. "Honey! Are you ready to eat?"

"Yeah, here I come right now."

Welma treated JC really good. She had fallen in love with him when she first saw him. That was three months ago before she moved him in. Welma was moving very fast with JC and he played along with it, loving every minute of her gift-giving. "Ok I'm about to take off to work, sweetie. I'll see you later tonight when I get off." She kissed him on the lips while he was at the table eating.

"Ok baby, thank you for breakfast."

"You welcome. I left you gas money on the dresser. Gas prices are going up and it's not cheap filling up that truck out there."

"Ok thank you and have a good day at work!"

JC finished up his food, eating every bit that was on his plate. When he was done washing his dish he went back to the room, turned on the computer and brought up his Facebook page. He had a lot of mail and comments. He opened a message from a lady named Jamie. A 48-year-old-black woman who was married, but obviously not happy. She had browsed JC's page and noticed that he liked older women.

Hi sexy, my name is Jamie, I browsed your page and I liked what I saw. I stay in the same area as you and it would be nice if I can get to know you a little better. Maybe I can meet you somewhere like the Mall in Dearborn. I wanted to leave you comments on your pictures, but I wasn't sure if you had a girl in your life. I saw that it said you were single, but I don't believe how a sexy man like you can be single. I loved looking at the picture you had on their showing your sexy body. You must work out.

Please message me back when you receive this. I really want to get to know you. I won't say a word as long as you don't. Love Jamie ... Check out my pictures on my page!

JC checked her page out to find a nice looking brown-skinned lady. She had about eight different pictures, all very revealing. He could tell she was a freak just by the pictures she had and the music she had playing when he first entered her page.

JC couldn't believe she was married and had a Facebook page. He was in love with the way Facebook worked. It was a mall, a club, a concert, a Superbowl game and a championship basketball game all in one.

CHAPTER 6

JC looked at the computer screen and saw that Jamie had just signed on. He figured he would reply back and possibly meet with her that day.

Hey, it's JC, I received your message today, I also checked out the pictures you displayed on your page, very nice! And of course I'm interested in meeting you. Just let me know when you have the time. Love JC

JC sent the message off, read his next messages, and the comments other females had left on his page. He scrolled back up the page and noticed that Jamie had written him back already.

Hi JC, I'm glad you returned my message, sweetheart. I'm available right now. If you want I can meet you at the mall. I would love to take you shopping, what do you say?

JC finished reading and was shocked at the kind of woman he just met. She wanted to take him shopping right this minute. He wasted no time replying.

Sure, that sounds good, I can be there in about 30 minutes. Meet me inside that restaurant called Carter's. Don't be late! Love JC

He quickly jumped in the shower and put on a nice expensive button-up, black and white, with some jet-black jeans and his all black boots. He made sure he signed off just in case Welma came home for some reason while he wasn't there. He drove all the way to Fairlane Mall in Dearborn. There was a nice crowd of people, but he still managed to find a parking spot close to the door. He parked the BMW and went into the restaurant.

"Can I help you, sir?" the waitress asked.

CHAPTER 7

J C was looking around the restaurant for his date, "Uhmm, I'm supposed to meet someone up here," he said to the waitress.

"Is it the lady over there in the corner?" she pointed.

JC wasn't sure. She looked a lot different from the pictures she had on her Facebook page.

"Yep, I think that is her," he said, following the waitress over to where Jamie was sitting. She was looking a lot better than her pictures.

"Hi, how you doing?" he asked, shaking her hand before he sat down right across from her.

She smiled, revealing pretty white teeth. "I'm fine, and you?"

"I'm good, just out enjoying this nice day."

"Awww, you're such a cutie pie."

"Thank you, were you hungry or –."

She cut him off, "No I'm not, I ate about an hour ago. Are you, because –?"

"No, I'm fine, I just ate too," he said, smiling.

"I already told you what I want to do. I wanna take you shopping!" she said excited.

He laughed, "You sure there's not any strings attached?"

She laughed. "No strings attached, mister, except for you to come home with me tonight and watch a movie, that's if you don't have anything on your agenda."

"Oh naw, that's fine. I can do that . . . Oh wait." JC had just remembered. "You said that you are married on your Facebook page, what's up with that? I ain't tryna get into no drama. I wouldn't ever put you in that situation, so I expect the same from me, if you don't mind."

Jamie looked right into his eyes as he talked. She was touched by the fact that he was only 21 years old but mature. She had dealt with men that were 25, 30 and older, and JC was by far more mature than most of them. She was used to guys usually not even asking her about her husband. They didn't care, they were just trying to get what they could from her . . . By JC asking her deep questions like that, she took it that, this wouldn't be something short-term.

"Yes, I am married. I live with my husband but right now he is out of town for the weekend and I wanna have fun."

CHAPTER 8

"So when does he come back?" JC asked.

"Monday morning. He's on a business trip."

"So are you saying this is a one time thing?"

That's the question Jamie was waiting for. Her plan was to take him shopping, bring him home and get her some young penis then cut him loose . . . Now she was starting to change her plans. JC was growing on her by the minute. *Maybe I can hold on to this depending on how good he is in bed. No way I'm going to keep wasting my money on a man that can't even move, let alone satisfy me,* she thought to herself.

"No, but I know you must have a woman you're in love with, I don't want to mess that up."

"I'm not in love but I do have someone that treats me very well. It takes time to fall in love, right?"

Jamie smiled at him. "Right . . . Boy, you something else, let's get out of here and tear down this mall!"

They both walked out and headed for the men's stores. Their first stop was a shoe store. Jamie picked up some white and blue shoes.

"You like these, JC?"

"Yeah them fresh," he said, walking up to her and examining the shoe. "I think these ones just came out too. Excuse me sir," he said to an employee that was busy adjusting the hats. "Are these the new arrivals?"

"Yup, we just got them in yesterday. We set them out this morning. Would you like a pair? What size do you need?" The salesperson didn't even give him a chance to answer if he even liked the shoe or not.

"Umm, let me get a 10 1/2 in these and a 10 1/2 in these all-white ones."

"Ok I'll be right back."

JC and Jamie walked around the shoe store looking for other stuff, but he didn't really see anything he really wanted. "Would this be all, sir?"

"Yup, that will be it."

"Would you like some socks?" The salesperson was trying to build his commission.

"Sure," Jamie said, pulling her credit card out of her purse.

"That will be $237.62," the clerk said as he swiped the credit card, gave them a receipt and sent them on their way. "Thanks for coming, have a great day."

"You too," Jamie said.

"I gotta pee, real quick," JC said.

"Can I help you?" Jamie asked smiling.

"Yup," he joked. Little did he know Jamie was serious.

He was in the bathroom for about two minutes before she walked in. The whole bathroom was empty except for the two of them. As soon as he saw her walking in, he almost pissed all over himself. "What you doing?" he whispered, now pushing his pee out as fast as he could.

"I wanna suck it for you."

"In here, are you serious?!"

"Yea, let's go into the last stall."

CHAPTER 9

They went into the biggest stall which was on the end. "You sure you wanna do this here?" JC whispered to her, nervously hoping she'd change her mind.

"Yeah relax, sit down or would you rather stand up?"

"I'll stand up, so you won't have to sit on the floor."

JC motioned for Jamie to sit on the toilet and she started unzipping his black jeans and pulled his penis out. *Wow!* she thought to herself, admiring his size on soft.

First, she kissed it softly then started using her tongue, licking his head at a fast speed. "Oh, shit," he whispered as his penis swelled up to it's maximum size of ten inches. She stroked him softly with her hand while putting half of his penis inside her mouth. She got it all wet and then deep throated the whole thing.

JC was shocked, as he had never had a female that could put the whole thing in her mouth. She kept him in her throat as she played with his balls with her hand which made him stand on his toes. "Oh shit, I'm cummin'," he whispered, not knowing whether to scream or pull away. "Oooh shit, wait wait!" he whispered, balling, his fist as he released what felt like buckets of sperm down her throat.

She swallowed it all while she still kept him in her mouth. JC was shaking and his knees were weak.

"Oh my god," he whispered as he tucked his penis back in his pants and zipped up. He couldn't believe how fast he came. Jamie knew what she was doing, and she wanted to let him know up front. They cautiously walked out the bathroom back into the mall. As they were walking out, a white man walked in, just staring but without saying anything. The next store they went in was an urban store, JC's favorite. They were in that store for about three hours. He tried on several different outfits with shoes. When they left, Jamie had charged up $4,657.62. He had so much stuff it was unbelievable. He was exhausted and figured Jamie had spent more than enough on him for the day. Hell, he probably could have had his own car instead of all that gear! They were walking out of the mall, JC carrying all the bags.

"May I escort you to your car?" he asked, being the gentlemen.

"Sure, are you going to follow me home?"

"Yep, I can do that."

They had parked in the same row which made things easier for JC because he was carrying a lot of bags. He walked her to her car, wondering what she was driving.

"Damn, that's you?" he asked, looking at the drop top white two-seater Cadillac XLR.

"Yes, it is. It's one of my four I own. You like?" She asked, with a coy smile.

"Hell yeah! This the shit!" he said, giving her mad props.

She laughed, "Thank you. How far away did you park?"

"Oh, I'm just a few cars down."

CHAPTER 10

JC walked to the SUV he was driving and started following Jamie back to her home. She was pretty sexy for her age and was in great shape. They had finally reached a Farmington Hills subdivision. All the houses had to cost a million and up. *Damn!* JC thought to himself. *This bitch loaded with money or her husband is.*

They pulled into the circle driveway where a few other nice cars were parked. Jamie had it made, and she knew it. She let the garage up to walk inside the house where two other expensive cars were.

"Come on JC, nobody's here but me and you," she said.

"I'm coming! I was just checking everything out," answered JC.

He walked through the garage into the house. The house had white carpeting all the way through. JC took his shoes off at the door. He was a little nervous about the whole situation. "Where are we going to watch the movie?"

"Upstairs in my room, do you drink? You want some Goose?" Jamie asked.

"Naw, I have to drive," JC said.

"You can sleep over, I don't mind," Jamie responded with a smile.

"I wish I could, but I can't. I'm driving someone else's car and I have to have it back at a certain time."

"Oh, JC that's fine, so you don't have a car?"

"Nope, not yet, I'm saving up for one right now."

"Well I'll help you save up for it. I'll give a thousand a month as long as you dick me down at least three times a month."

"That's a deal!" JC said. He was shocked that she approached him that way. JC had discovered a gold mine and she was definitely willing to help him. She was loving his little swag he had going on. He carried himself like an older man and that's what she liked.

"So, what movie do you want me to watch with you?" he asked, sitting on the bar stool, checking out the marble countertop.

"It's a surprise, follow me."

They went upstairs to the master bedroom. Her room was done in all white. A big jacuzzi tub sat in the middle of the floor and a nice king size bed was not far from it. "Damn, this is nice!"

"Thank you, I know you're on a time limit, so I'm going to speed things up for you."

JC watched her walk to the flat screen where she put a DVD on, a porno. She dimmed the lights and made it almost dark in the whole room. Then she clicked the switch to the Jacuzzi and it started up. Jamie finished her drink of liquor then used the remote to turn on some slow music. She had set the mood, and JC was used to it; all he messed around with was older women. They both started taking off their clothes as they kissed with mostly their tongues. They both were naked and soon he laid her down, taking control as he started kissing her around her navel.

CHAPTER 11

Her vagina was nicely shaved, just perfect. He planted nice, gentle, soft kisses all the way down to her thighs, while she spread her legs, ready to feel his aggressive tongue on her clit. He continued kissing all the way down her legs to her beautiful feet. Kissing each toe one at a time, he then started sucking two at a time. Jamie's eyes were rolling as she was rubbing her own titties, moaning and rotating her hips. He started on her other foot, bathing each toe with his warm saliva. Her juices were flowing like crazy. He was even able to see the puddle that she made while he was sucking her toes.

He swirled his tongue back up her soft thighs, kissing them slowly as he felt her motioning towards him almost forcing him to lick her pussy, but he still made her wait a little longer. "JC please!" Jamie cried out, breathing hard. "Please, just give it to me!" She couldn't take the tease anymore, she was ready to feel him. He bit softly between her thighs all the way up to her clit.

Then he spread her lips with his two fingers and started licking like a machine. She screamed out as her body immediately started shaking while she came hard and long. "I wanna ride your face," she said in a sultry voice, begging for more. They got into the 69 position, with her on top. He put his arms under her legs, wrapping them around her so she couldn't run away from what he was about to give her. He had her butt cheeks spread wide open as he went to work with his strong tongue on her warm, wet pussy.

As he was pleasuring her, she was returning the favor by putting both of his balls in her mouth, juggling them with her tongue. The more electricity he sent through her body with his tongue, the more she sent back. It was like she was trying to choke herself, the way she was sucking his penis. The two were in ecstasy, ready to explode. Jamie was trying to pull away, but he kept pulling her back.

"Oh shit JC, I'm about to cum!" she yelled, grinding harder on his face and still sucking him hard. "Baby cum with me!" she moaned. "Cum in my mouth, baby!" she yelled, sucking him harder until he exploded all over her mouth, and that's when she drew the whole thing down into her throat, but still she was moving her pussy up and down on his tongue until she came all over his face.

CHAPTER 12

They both were shaking, and their bodies were limp. They started being extra gentle with one another, switching positions as he laid on top of her, kissing her neck and ears, pulling her hair and kissing her on the mouth. Grinding against each other, he was still-rock hard when she grabbed him and slid him inside of her. He felt so warm caressing her insides with his long, rock-hard penis.

"Baby, you feel so good," she moaned, digging her nails into his back while she rotated her hips slowly. He pumped her slowly and passionately, going deeper inside her warm pussy. She wasn't loose, she wasn't tight, she was just right. She rolled him over so she could get on top, putting his full ten inches inside of her. She started to move her hips faster and faster, feeling herself about to cum again, moaning, "cum with me JC, cum with me." She kept on rolling her hips, moving her body like a hungry snake, grinding harder, shaking uncontrollably and squeezing her pussy muscles causing him to cum with her.

"Oh baby," he said, breathing hard.

"Fuuuuck!"

Jamie laid on top of JC until they caught their breath. "You like this pussy, JC?" she asked, grinding slowly on top of him with sweat glistening all over her body.

"Yeah I like this pussy! You feel so good," he replied, slowly grinding back, still shaking from the nut he had just bust.

"You like cummin' in this pussy?" she asked, licking her lips and sucking her teeth.

"Yes baby."

"You gonna cum in this pussy again for me, JC?"

"Yes baby."

"You promise, baby!" she asked moaning, looking deeply into JC's eyes.

"I promise baby! You feel so good!" he moaned out as he came deep inside her again. They both were breathing hard and their hearts were pounding harder.

CHAPTER 13

Welma got off work at 9 p.m. She had been calling JC's cell phone and not getting an answer. *What the hell is he doing?* she thought to herself. *He better not have nobody in my house.* She tried calling him again and still no answer. *Maybe he can't hear his cell phone ringing. I'll call the house phone.* She dialed her house phone number and the phone rang twice before JC answered it.

"Hello."

"What you are doing?"

"Nothing, chillin' on the computer."

"You on that Facebook shit again?"

He laughed, "Naw I ain't messing with that right now."

"Yeah right, I know your lil self on there searching for them young girls."

"What I need them for? I got you honey, Now hurry your ass home before I kick your ass," he joked.

She laughed, "Boy please! And why the hell you not answering your cell phone?"

"Lady stop asking so many questions. Just get here, sexy. Bye." He hung the phone up.

All Welma could do was laugh. *That boy knows he crazy*, she thought to herself.

JC was chillin back at the condo, having phone sex with Jamie. That's why he wasn't answering his cell phone for Welma when she was calling. "So, when can I see you again?"

"It will be pretty soon. My husband is coming back, so it might be a little harder to get away, but I'll figure something out."

"Ok sounds good. Well, I'll talk to you later then, I'm about to go to sleep. You wore me out today."

She laughed, "Whatever! Shooot you wore *me* out!" They both laughed. "Ok boy, I'll talk to you later. Be good and good night."

"Ok bye baby. Goodnight."

The next morning JC signed on to Facebook right after Welma left for work. She had made him breakfast before leaving, like always. Today she drove the BMW to work and left him the Lexus.

JC was still in his boxers on the computer. As soon as he signed on, he noticed he had new comments, picture comments, new friend requests and new messages. *What should I check first?* he thought to himself. *New friend request,* he clicked. There were seven different people that wanted to be his friend. He clicked on the first girl.

She was 19 years old, from Pontiac. He scrolled down her page a little to see what her occupation was and where she was going to college. She was a Leo, and she was going to cosmetologist. JC scrolled back up to check out her friend list.

A total of 612 friends. He scrolled back up and clicked her pictures. She had about four pages of pictures posted. There were pictures of her and her friends at the club. She was nice looking, light skin, long hair. She looked like she was mixed with something, plus she had a nice body. JC clicked back to his friend request and clicked on *Confirm*. Now she was on his friend list and he was on hers. Since they were friends now, they could send comments to each other and comment on each other's pictures. JC now had 1097 friends. He clicked back to the girl's page and added a comment.

Thank you for the add, get at me sexy.

CHAPTER 14

He went back to his page to his friend request and looked at the second person that was asking to be his friend. It was a dude, and he was from New York. He had a music page. JC browsed his page and saw that he had eight songs he composed himself. JC had never heard of him, but he still accepted him as a friend. The guy had close to ten thousand friends. JC clicked back to his page to see his third friend request. Another girl, so he clicked on her, but she was only 15. "Aw, hell naw!" He went back to his page and denied her as a friend. Not that she was ugly, but the little girl was only fifteen asking to be friends with a 21- year-old guy! JC went back to look at his next friend request. It was his cousin from Kentucky. He accepted him and sent him a comment also.

What up cuz? How you been doing?

He clicked back to his page and saw that he had two more new friend requests plus the other three. The ones that were girls he accepted. The other two that were guys he denied. Now he had 1,103 friends on his friend list. He clicked back to view his picture comments. *Three new picture comments.* All of the comments were about the picture where he had his shirt off.

1. Damn baby you sexy!

2. Let me lick your body....

3. Can I cuddle with you, sexy?

Each comment was left by a different sexy woman. Each in their early 20's. He clicked on the first one. He had remembered chatting with her a couple months back and she was lame plus she was so far from Michigan. He could have flirted back but instead he just left her a regular comment.

Thanks for the picture comment.

CHAPTER 15

Then he clicked back to the second comment. It was from a white girl from Southfield, 26 years old. *Oh I remember her,* he thought to himself. He had already had sex with her a while back when she first asked to be his friend. He clicked on her pictures to show some love back. She had a new picture, one where she was lying on a bed with a big white t-shirt and a red thong on. He clicked on that picture to post a comment.

Damn baby, you still looking sexy, when can I lay next to you again?

At first, he wasn't going to add the word again because he didn't know if she wanted her business out there like that. But he figured, since she's on here with a thong on, she must not have a man. Plus, if she didn't like the comment he wrote, she could erase it anyway. JC went to the third picture comment.

Again, this was someone he had met in the past. He remembered trying to sleep with her before, but she was playing games, not even wanting to return his message. Now possibly, she was trying to get with him, unless she was just bored when she left that comment. All her pictures were professional. She was 23 years old and she was Puerto Rican with a big booty and long hair. *I guess I'll reply to this,* he thought. Since she asked a question like that, he figured he will reply back through an email. He hoped she would reply right back because she was online right now. He went to her page and clicked on send message.

Yeah you can cuddle with me baby whenever you ready, just holla at me on here or call me at 313-555-2361. Love JC Don't be a stranger. He sent that message to her then continued to browse his page.

He scrolled down to see his new comments.

Hey baby how you been, I miss you, get at me when you have time, one girl wrote.

What up pimp? another wrote.

What up my dog? I see you got all the females on your page, hook me up! A dude wrote, his name was Marvin, he was always leaving JC messages. JC accepted him as a friend a month ago. Just because he let him be his friend on Facebook, doesn't mean he wanted him to be a friend he hung out with outside of Facebook.

Thanx for the add, a pretty white girl wrote.

Those were all his new comments since yesterday when he was online. Last but not least, he checked his messages.

CHAPTER 16

JC had about five new messages in his inbox. He clicked on his new messages and saw that it was from Jamie.

Hi baby, I miss you already. I need some more of that big dick of yours. You were great, I wish my husband can give it to me like that, but I guess he getting too old because since I've been with him, he never moved like you did. Maybe we can meet up tomorrow for a quick second, because I forgot to give you some money to put away for your car, so call me when you have time on my cell phone. Love Jamie, Good night.

Jamie must've sent that message after they got off the phone last night. He didn't reply to it, but just planned on calling her in the afternoon. He went to his second message, which was from the girl he had just sent his phone number to. He clicked on the message.

Boy, you couldn't handle me if you tried, I hope your pockets looking right playboy because I stay ready, so you holla at me when you ready. I'll text my number to your phone.

Aw hell naw! he thought to himself, *this bitch got me fucked up. I don't pay for sex, I get paid for sex!* He didn't even reply to her message because it was obvious that she was a gold-digger looking for a handout. Two gold-diggers of the opposite sex won't work unless they are working with each other as a team. *Fuck that Ho'!* He went to his third message. It was a female he hadn't talked to in a while. He had changed his number and moved in with Welma, and she hadn't seen him in months. She didn't know what happened to him but found him on Facebook.

Bitch, you think you slick, you sneaky muthafucka! You a nasty muthafucka, when I see you, I'm shooting you, you grimy-ass bitch! You knew you got me pregnant, so you ran away! Yea, I'm getting an abortion because I don't want my baby having a sorry, deadbeat, punk-ass daddy like you, you ain't shit! You thought you could hide, you stupid muthafucka? I know where you been staying at too. I'mma come blow all them windows out too!

CHAPTER 17

JC didn't even finish reading the message that Rita wrote. She was tripping. *Damn, I had her pregnant,* he said to himself. He thought about replying but instead dialed her number private. She picked up after four rings.

"Who calling me private?"

"This is JC."

"You stupid muthafucka! You think this is a fucking game, leaving me knocked up and changing your number! When I see —."

JC interrupted all the yelling she was doing. "Calm down! Calm ya' dumb ass down, before I hang up!"

She thought about what he said and calmed down. If he hung up on her, she wouldn't have been able to call him back because he blocked the number and she would rather talk to him on the phone versus sending him messages on Facebook. "Ok go ahead J fucking C! The man with the master plan!" she joked.

He laughed at her sarcasm. "Look Rita, it ain't even got to be like this, I didn't even know you were pregnant."

"You knew I wasn't on birth control and you had been nutting in me since you had been home from prison! What you thought, nothing was going to happen?"

"Naw man, this what happened," he said, thinking of a good lie. "A tragedy happened in my family, so I went out of town for a while. I ain't trying to beef with you. You talking about you going to bust out somebody's windows, chill that shit out. And to pop your little ass bubble, I'm staying in Kentucky right now. Maybe if you chill out, I'll come see you soon and give you some of this get-right you been missing out on!" He had lied about the tragedy and about being in Kentucky, but it was working.

"Aww, I'm sorry to hear that, I ain't mean to go off like that, I was just tripping because I'm missing you so much and I haven't seen or talked to you in months. All I want to do is see you."

"Well, fly me in, and I'll come see you. I miss you too."

"How much is it?"

"Just go to the bank and deposit $500 in my account. That should be enough to fly me there and to get a rental car."

"Ok I will. Just give me a few hours. Call me back later today, don't forget. It ain't like I can call you, being that you blocked your number."

"I won't forget. I'll call you, but make sure nobody knows I'm coming."

"Ok boo, I promise I won't tell, bye. Bye."

"Bye girl."

CHAPTER 18

He hung up the phone, laughing to himself. He had just talked her into $500 for a plane ticket, and he was only about an hour away. *Good thing she don't know none of my family members.* JC continued to check his messages and replied to them. He also replied to the comments people left on his page. When he was done, he started searching for a new cougar. He kept it in a fifty-mile radius meaning he was looking for someone no farther than an hour away. Then he typed in 32-55 years old, all females, black, white, or Latino, height didn't matter, single or married. A big list of pictures popped upon the screen giving him 3,000 different pages to look at. That's roughly 90,000 different women. He scrolled down, checking out the most attractive pictures, then double-clicking on the one that caught his eye the most. Browsing her page, saw that she was 35 years old, single, a Virgo, and made between $100,000-$250,000 a year. a lot of people lie about the money they make, so you couldn't let that get you excited. He scrolled down to check more out. He noticed she only had 24 friends total. Either she didn't really know how to work Facebook, she was new to Facebook, or she didn't log on much. Whatever the reason was, JC was going to find out. She was a nicely dressed lady. All her pictures were casual. She was a very pretty woman in the face, plus she was online right now. *I gotta pop at her and see what's up,* JC thought to himself, then he sent her a message.

Hi beautiful, my name is JC, are you new to Facebook? Because I never seen you on here before? Just curious, w/b.

JC just sent a simple note trying to see where her head was. He didn't want to be too aggressive and didn't want to be disrespectful. He had to be patient on this one. She could be a winner and plus where she stayed wasn't too far from him.

CHAPTER 19

JC's Vanessa received JC's message. She was at work but wasn't busy she was never busy. All she did was sit in an office all day at a nice desk with a computer and phone. Before she replied back, she checked on his page. She thought he was a handsome man, but young. *Twenty-one years old, he's still a baby!* she thought, scrolling down his page. Then a song popped on. It was her favorite song, "Separated" by Avant. JC was smooth. Before he sent her a message, he changed his song to the same song she had on her page. Now she was thinking about writing him back. *He don't seem like 21 years old, we even got the same song on our page, what can he possibly know about that song?* She began browsing his page, looking at his comments, all females. *A li'l player I see!* She thought as she read his comments.

Vanessa kept scrolling and reading. *This boy has too many females chasing him. Well, I can write him back, he only asked me if I was new to Facebook,* she thought to herself.

Hi JC, I'm Vanessa, yes, I am kind of new to this, thanks for the

compliment. What your little young self know about that song?
"Vanessa"

JC had been waiting for Vanessa to write back. She was taking a while, so in the meantime he was browsing other cougars. If one doesn't bite, go on to the next, that was his game. He noticed that Vanessa had written him back, so he replied. *You're welcome Vanessa. That's a gorgeous name, you have the same name as my little sister. . . What I know about that song? A lot, that's my song right there, you want me to sing it to you?* "JC"

JC didn't even know how to sing. He was just trying to get his foot in the door.

Vanessa had received his message. *What! No he didn't just ask to sing it to me.* She laughed and went back to his page. *Let me check this lil fella out.* She clicked on his pictures and scrolled down. *Damn, he got a nice body and he handsome,* I could braid his hair, she laughed, trying to think of a way to give into him without him noticing. She wasn't thinking about having sex with him, she just didn't mind chatting with him. He was a cool respectful young man she thought, so she wrote him back.

Boy how old are you? Are you really 21? You don't look like it. Thanks again for the compliment about my name. Oh you can sing? I'd love to hear you. One more question... Who braids your hair? Just write me back and I'll get back to you later. I'm about to go on my lunch break. "Vanessa"

Vanessa sent her message with a smile then grabbed her purse and left the office to go get something to eat.

CHAPTER 20

JC took care of everything he had to take care of while Welma was at work. He had met up with Jamie and she gave him the $1,000 she promised. He made his way to the bank to check his account and Rita had already deposited the $500. Now it was time for him to call her. "Hey boo!" she answered, excited.

"How you know it was me?"

"Because you the only asshole that calls me blocked!"

"Oh, ok," he laughed.

"You get your plane ticket yet?" she asked.

"Yeah, I should be there by 11:00."

"Yes! I'm so pumped, I can't wait to see you."

"Same here. I got a rental too, so I should be at your house by 11:45 tonight."

"Ok daddy, I'll be waiting."

"Yeah, be naked for me, I wanna stick my dick right inside you as soon as I get in the door."

"Ooh daddy! My pussy dripping right now."

"Alright, well, see you later."

"Ok bye-bye." He hung up the phone and called Welma. Her phone rang about seven times. "Hello, hi baby," she said.

"What you doing?"

"Umm...working, why?"

"Because I'm missing you! What time are you going to be home to see me?"

"Aww! I miss you too, sweetheart, but I won't be home until about 1:30 a.m. It's Saturday. You know I go to my friend's house to play cards and party."

"Ok well whenever you get home I'll be waiting for you, I'mma eat that pussy up for you late ok?"

She smiled hard, laughing, "Ok JC, I'll see you later. Bye."

He hung up then drove back to the condo. He jumped in the shower and put on one of the outfits Jamie bought him. He threw on a blue and white outfit, put on his expensive cologne, then jumped on the computer to burn some time until 11:00p.m. He signed on Facebook for the second time that day. He had only new messages.

He clicked on his messages and saw that Vanessa had written him earlier. He read her message, *damn I think I got this one,* he thought after reading it and then replied.

"I'm 21, Vanessa, I wouldn't lie to you. A lot of people always tell me that I look and act older than my age. You're welcome, it's a beautiful name. Your question was, who braids my hair? Well no one right now, I go to the salon. But I'm looking for someone that can braid, I'll pay you... Let me know, because I need my hair done ASAP and I don't have 85 dollars to spend on some braids right now, so let me know something soon, and maybe I can teach you how to work Facebook. "JC"

JC sent the message knowing she wouldn't reply until later that night or whenever she went back to work. He remembered that if Rita were to sign on, he might get questioned because he's supposed to be on a plane. He continued to do his thing online and time flew by. It was 10:58 p.m. when he looked at the clock. He turned off the computer and went out the door. Leaving Romulus and driving all the way to Flint took him only an hour at the speed he was going. As soon as he entered the city, he called Rita from his cell phone.

"Where are you boy? I'm getting sleepy."

"I'm pulling up right now baby and start saying *hello* first when you pick up the phone," he added.

"I do, just not to blocked calls."

"Come open the door."

"You outside?"

"Um yeah, come open the door."

"Here I come." She hung up the phone, and ran to her door to let JC in.

CHAPTER 21

When he saw Rita, she was looking as sexy as always, resembling the famous Vivica Fox in the face and Buffy in the waist. She was still looking good but was just crazy. A drama queen and he hated it. She kept herself in beef with other women over JC even when they weren't messing around. JC did regret getting her pregnant because he knew she would keep it. She tried to lie to him, but he knew her ways far too well.

JC had to get this done quickly, so he immediately lifted her up and started kissing her. She wrapped her legs around him and put her arms around his neck. "Baby I miss you so much," she whispered, still kissing him aggressively and sucking his bottom lip. He led her to the bed and began taking his clothes off. He laid his 9mm pistol on the bed. Rita didn't think anything of him having a gun because she was used to seeing him with one. She slid her panties off and then her bra. She pulled JC on top of her. Her heart was pounding because she had been missing him for so long. Her pussy was dripping wet just from his presence. She could not believe JC had come back to her. This time she was going to do her best to keep things perfect with him. She was going to do anything he wanted too. He was the man of her dreams.

JC slid against her warm body, kissing her neck. She smelled as good as always. She quickly gripped his long hard penis with her soft hands and shoved it inside her, ignoring the pain. She was so warm and wet, her juices were flowing out her fast. It was like he was dipping in a water puddle as she was splashing everywhere, every time he went deep. It felt so good to him, but he didn't have much time.

"Turn over baby, I want to hit it from the back," he said, helping her get into a doggy-style position. He quickly re-entered her and she moaned out for him to go deeper, gripping him with the muscles inside her. He pumped slowly, hitting every little spot. He reached over to his pistol, which was already cocked and ready. He started pulling her hair and pounding her super hard, making her scream louder, then he pulled the trigger, shooting her directly in the back of the head. Her screams immediately stopped as she fell to the bed, covered in blood, with pieces of her brain splattered around her. He took her cell phone, and proceeded to destroy her computer drive, he then pulled her off her bed, wrapped in her bed sheets and dumped her body in the closet. He quickly headed for the exit, locking every door behind him.

He made it back to the condo before Welma came home. He had taken a hot shower and laid in the bed, falling to sleep within minutes.

CHAPTER 22

JC woke up to the smell of pancakes, eggs and bacon. Welma cooked him breakfast every morning. It was Sunday and she didn't have to work, and he didn't either. "Good morning, boo," she said, holding a tray with a plate of food on it. She slid it onto his lap and gave him a kiss on the lips.

"Thank you, boo."

"What you want to drink, milk or orange juice?"

"Umm, I'll have some milk please."

"Ok." she said and walked out of the room in her sexy see-through robe. She had such a nice body- no stretch marks, dimples or cellulite. She always had on different kinds of sexy robes when she was around the house. She knew she had to stay sexy for her man. And under her robes she always wore an expensive pantie set.

"Here you go," she said, setting his milk down on the

nightstand beside him. "So, you going to show me how to setup my page on Facebook today?" she smiled, turning on the television.

He smiled and looked at her. "What you gonna do with a Facebook page?"

"The same thing you do. I'm going to get my pimp on and find me some friends to chat with every day like you."

"Babe, chill out, you don't need no Facebook page."

"You got one, why you don't want me to have one?"

He took a bite of his bacon, "It's not that I don't want you to have one, it's just that I don't think you need one, unless you saying you getting bored with me."

She laughed, "Boy you need to stop! You know I'm not getting bored with you, I'm just curious about why you on there every day for hours?"

"Baby it's just something to do, what you rather me go out to clubs or something?"

"No, stick with Facebook," she said looking at the television.

He laughed, "What you so curious and worried about baby?"

She was still looking straight ahead at the T.V.

"Welma."

"What!" she turned and looked at him.

"You heard me."

"Yeah, I heard you... I'm not."

"You not what?"

"I'm not worried or curious about anything, JC."

"You sure?"

"Yes JC."

"Well stop acting so weird, like I'm cheating on you or something."

"You done?" she asked, reaching for the tray.

"Yeah, that was good, thank you baby."

"You welcome." She took the tray to the kitchen and came back to the room to lie down with him. "I've missed you so much."

"I've missed you too," he said, pulling her close and kissing her soft lips.

CHAPTER 23

She started rubbing him, from his chest down past his abs to the inside of his boxers. "Aww, he's sleeping," she joked, wrapping her hands around his soft penis. "Naw, I'm not even gonna get you started," she laughed. "JC, I have a question."

"What is it?" he asked kissing her on her forehead.

"I'm serious, JC and I need you to be completely honest."

"Ok Welma, what is it."

"I wanna know, how you feel about me?"

"What kind of question is that boo? You know I love you with all my heart and would never do anything to hurt you. I want to be with you and only you."

Welma didn't say anything, but just pulled herself closer to him and held him tighter. "So, you sure you not messing around with other females?"

"See there you go, you don't even trust me."

"Yes I do JC, I do trust you."

"Well, why you keep saying stuff like that?"

"Because I don't want you to leave me for anybody else. If I'm not doing something right, let me know and I'll fix it. I just want to be the one to make you happy."

"Baby you doing everything right, I ain't going nowhere."

They laid there silently watching DVD's all day. Welma had made lunch and dinner for them both. Around nine o'clock that night she dozed off to sleep because she had to be at work in the morning.

JC had to go to work as well, but not until seven o'clock later that evening. As soon as he noticed that Welma was sleeping, he went to the computer and noticed that he had new messages and friend requests. He first clicked on his friend requests. A pretty white girl had requested to be his friend and she was online. He quickly accepted her, not even having to go to her page to see more pictures. He went to her layout page and scrolled down noticing that she had 2,300 friends total. *Damn, she do this shit,* he thought to himself. She was a college student at Oakland University. He quickly scrolled down to send her a comment.

Thanx for the add sexy, get at me.

Then he scrolled up to click on her pictures, of which she had about twelve and that's all he needed to see. *She's 24 years old and single with no kids, and fine as hell!* Her body was banging, and she was built like a black woman. *Goddamn!* he said to himself, trying not to be too loud because Welma was sleeping. He was checking out a picture of her in some red stretch pants and a bra. He could see her whole figure.

She was definitely fine, and JC wanted her, so he clicked back to his page to see if she had returned his comment.

You welcome Mr... Thanks for the compliment. She had already returned his comment. That was a good sign, especially being that she came at him first by requesting him as a friend.

How you doing? My name is JC...You should let me get to know you a little better as a friend, if that's Ok with you. "JC"

CHAPTER 24

Kelly received his message. She loved black men, but she had only been with two her whole life. The first one was shot and killed. She had been with him since she was 14 years old and he was one of only two guys she had ever had sex with. That's at least what she told everyone she met. He taught her everything she knew and that day she was admiring the way JC looked, so she messaged him back.

I'm doing fine, how about yourself? As friends? Sounds perfect, I'm not trying to start anything serious right now, but there's nothing wrong with friends . . . Don't start thinking otherwise. I did read your page and noticed all the groupies, so I know you are a little player, but I'm just letting you know up front, that I'm totally different, I don't just have sex just to be having it with any and everybody... Oh, my name is Kelly btw. "Kelly"

JC read her message. *Damn, straight up?* he messaged her right back.

I'm fine, also, damn why you gotta cut into me like that? Shit,

I'm different too, I ain't just trying to get in your panties baby. I'm really trying to find out why you so beautiful with no man . . ."JC"

Ok I'm sorry JC, I didn't mean it like that. Stop being so sensitive! LOL . . . It's just that so many guys on here message me on straight bullshit. They are disrespectful on here. I just thought you were that kind. "Kelly"

I accept your apology, I feel where you coming from, even though you went off on me. I'm getting scared of you all ready. LOL "JC"

OMG, I didn't go off on you. Stop making me feel bad. I'm not mean at all, I promise! "Kelly"

Ok I guess I'll believe you for now . . . so, what do you like doing? Tell me a little about yourself. "JC"

I'm not the outdoor type, I like staying at home, I watch a lot of movies and I take college classes online for Small Business Entrepreneurship. How about you? "Kelly"

I chill most of the time, I don't go out much either. If you don't mind, my number is 313-555-2361. You can call me right now, I don't do much typing. I'd rather talk on the phone. "JC"

Ok I'm going to program your number in my phone right now. I have somewhere to be early in the morning, so I'm about to go to bed, but I'll definitely call you tomorrow. Maybe we can do lunch. "Kelly"

CHAPTER 25

T he next morning JC received a call from an unknown number, "Hello."

"Hello, is JC available?"

"Speaking, may I ask who's calling?"

"This is Kelly! How are you?"

"Oh, what's up Kelly? I'm good, how about you?"

"I'm fine, just out doing a little house shopping."

"Oh ok, where you on your way to? Maybe we can meet up."

"That sounds good, where do you want to meet? I'm all the way in Saginaw coming south on I-75."

"Ok do you know where Auburn Hills is?"

"Yes, I know where it is."

"How about we meet at the Palace? Then we'll go from there,

how that sounds?"

"Sounds good, but I'm going to be about an hour and a half."

"Ok that's fine, I'll meet you there around noon."

"Ok don't be late, playa!" she laughed.

"Why I gotta be a playa?"

"Just kidding, I'll see you at noon."

"Ok bye."

"Bye."

JC hung up his phone then headed for the shower. Welma was already at work for the day, and he had to go in at 7:00 p.m. After he was done taking a shower he got dressed, putting on one of his new outfits. He sprayed on his cologne and looked in the mirror.

Damn, it's about to be time for some new braids in a minute, he thought to himself. He had a little time left before he headed out, so he logged onto Facebook to see if Vanessa had written him back yet. He scrolled up, clicking on his messages. One new message from Vanessa.

Ok I believe you, and yes I'll braid your hair, no problem, whenever you ready call me at 313-555-7001. Make sure you call after 3:00 because I'm usually working before that. Just to let you know, I do not give my number out on the Internet to nobody, especially young men, so please don't make me hurt you. LOL. Just kidding, I won't hurt you. Call me. "Vanessa"

After reading her message, he saved her number in his cell phone and planned to call her later. He then signed off and went out the door, heading for Auburn Hills.

CHAPTER 26

Kelly was already just a few minutes away from the Palace. She had to stop in Pontiac to pick up some money first, but she was going to make it on time. She owned a five-bedroom house in Pontiac that had just recently been remodeled. Five women that worked for her were staying there. She ran something like an escort service, but it was a little different. This was an exotic cleaning service. She had two men that were nicely built that drove her girls to whatever job they had lined up. Kelly paid each girl $15.00 an hour plus she paid for their housing. She also bought all their costume and lingerie sets. A customer was not allowed to touch. All he or she could do was look. Business was good and Kelly received no complaints. Her target market was older, wealthy men. She had someone in charge of each of the two houses she ran. All she had to do was pick up money every morning.

"Hi Rich," Kelly said to her brother while giving him a hug.

"What's up, sis?" He said handing her a white envelope with money in it.

"How's everything going?"

"It's good, business stays good in the exotic world."

They both laughed.

"I'm going to need you to be here around 2:00 p.m. Our new vehicles should be here." Kelly had leased two Yukon SUV'S in her business name. Both of the Yukon's were all black with standard equipment, just to better her business image.

"Ok I'll be here, no problem. What did you get?"

"You'll see when they get here."

He laughed, "Aww, don't do me like that?"

"Ok I got two Yukon's, brand new."

"Oh, ok that sounds good."

"Well, I'll see you tomorrow, I have to be somewhere."

"Ok sis. Well be careful, I love you."

"Love you, too."

CHAPTER 27

JC was waiting in the Palace parking lot, ten minutes early scanning for Kelly. He sat there for a minute listening to the radio until he saw a pearl colored Escalade pull up. *Damn, is that her!* he wondered as his phone rang. "Hello."

"Hi, this is Kelly. I'm at the Palace, where are you?"

"I'm looking right at you. I'm in the silver BMW truck."

"Oh, ok I see you. Here I come."

Kelly pulled up next to JC and stepped out of the vehicle. *Damn! She is banging!* JC thought. Kelly was wearing a pair of white stretch Capri pants, sandal heels, a black and white halter top with gold earrings and expensive gold wire frames. She looked perfect.

"Damn baby, you are looking good!"

"Thank you. You are too," she said, giving him a hug.

"You're welcome and thank you."

"You are welcome, too. So, have you eaten yet?" she asked.

"A few hours ago, but I can go again."

"Ok good, because I'm SOOO hungry. I haven't eaten all day."

"What are you in the mood for?"

"Let's eat at Butter Bun," she said smiling. "You ever heard of that?"

Damn, she has pretty teeth, pretty feet, a pretty face and the perfect body. Something has to be wrong with this girl, he thought. "No, what's that?"

"A restaurant not too far away from here. Try it, I promise it's good."

"Ok let's go. Do you want me to drive or you?"

"I'll drive," she said.

They jumped inside Kelly's truck and drove to the restaurant.

"Whose truck are you driving?"

"This is mine, honey. I work hard for mine," she said smiling. Kelly was a classy white girl, but she also had some "hood" in her.

"Oh, ok. I see, I see, that's good. Where did you say you worked again?" he asked wondering what kind of job earns well enough to pay for an Escalade.

"I run my own cleaning service."

"Ok that's what's up!" JC didn't go any further into it. *Her cleaning service must be doing good,* he thought.

JC and Kelly listened to music the rest of the way to the

restaurant. She was clearly admiring JC, she found him laid back and real cool. Didn't bore, irritate or make her mad in any type of way. They hit it off really well.

"Hi, how many will be eating today?"

"Just two, please," Kelly said with a smile.

"Smoking or non-smoking?"

"Do you smoke?"

"No, do you?"

"No, I don't . . . non-smoking, please."

"Ok" the waitress answered. They followed the waitress to the table.

"What will you guys be drinking today?"

"I'll have lemonade please," Kelly said smiling.

"I'll have the same, thank you," JC said.

"Ok" the waitress said. "I'll be right back."

They were admiring each other, and they had so much in common. JC had never been serious with a white girl before, but this one was different. She was smart, fine, single, had no kids and she had it going on. He had to hold on to this one. She was a keeper.

CHAPTER 28

"So how many dates have you had with guys on Facebook?"

She laughed, "How many dates or how many guys?"

"Guys."

"This month or –?"

JC laughed, "Wow! Ok, ok I see. And you called me a pimp? You're the pimp!"

She laughed, "No I am not, I swear, I go out with them and usually, I can tell if I'm interested in that person or not."

"So how many guys are you feeling right now?"

"Other than you just one, but he has four kids by two different women and that's too much drama."

"Ya'll fucking?"

"No!"

"Whatever."

"I swear, I'm not!"

"So, what is it between you and him? I ain't trying to get shot, fucking with you."

She laughed because he looked so serious. "JC. . . you are not going to get shot messing around with me. Unless you piss me off, then I'll be doing the shooting."

JC squinted his eyes.

"I'm just kidding!" she joked, laughing.

"See, I have to watch you. You crazy," he joked back. They both laughed.

"Are you guys ready to order yet?"

"Yes, I'll have the pancake special, with scrambled eggs and bacon please," Kelly said.

"I'll have the same with a side of strawberries and whipped cream, please."

"Ok will that be all?"

"Yes," Kelly replied

"Yup," JC added.

"Ok it'll be just a few minutes."

"Ok."

"Why do you keep doing what I do?" Kelly asked.

JC laughed, "I can't help it if we like the same things. I really wanted grits, but I didn't see them on the menu."

She laughed, "They don't serve grits here."

"It's fine. I'm satisfied just being here with you right now."

"How sweet."

They continued to talk and eat their breakfast and then Kelly dropped him off at his car and he got his first kiss from her. Just a peck but it all works. JC knew this girl would be hard to get close to. He would really have to play a full-time roll with her. She was the type that would have to know his whereabouts to make sure he's serious with her. He could tell she wasn't about games, so if he wanted her, he had a lot of straightening up to do. Before he did that though, he needed to do his own investigating about her first, to make sure she was worth straightening up for.

CHAPTER 29

J C had been back on the streets for almost a year now.

He had done two years in prison for two ounces of cocaine. Definitely not worth the time. But for all the cocaine he did get away with, two years wasn't a problem. While he did his time, he worked out most of the time, read books and talked to O.G's about females and life. He didn't have parents or family that he knew of. His father was dead, and his mom had given him up at birth to foster care because she was so young. She was 14 years old when she had him. A foster care worker had found him in the back of their building in a trash can, crying. He found a home at the age of six, but by 13, he was in the juvenile system. In and out until he was 16 years old. At 17, he did nine months in the county jail and when he turned 18, he went to prison for two years. His foster parents disowned him by then because of the trouble he kept getting into. They couldn't control him, and they were done trying. Most of his life he had been locked up, so he had to grow up quick. He had too many drug cases on his record already and didn't ever want to go back to prison for drugs.

He was only supposed to do one year in prison, but the parole board flopped him for having sex with Rita in the visiting room . . . He was lucky on that situation, because they could have given him another charge. His mom was still around but she had changed her name. JC knew how bad his mother did him at birth, but he still wanted to reunite with her. He had forgiven her and promised that he would look for her when he was released from prison.

He hadn't started looking yet because he was trying to get his life together, but ever since he had been with Welma, she had made things a lot easier, even getting him a job where she worked. Facebook was the best thing besides Welma in his life right now. He was on parole for a couple of more months, so he still had to be careful. He wasn't going back to prison. That's why he had to stop talking to Rita. She was crazy and full of drama. Her next move would probably have been to call his parole officer, trying to get him locked up again, so he had to get rid of her quick. He had about five other friends he needed to pay back as well.

The whole time he was locked up, they hadn't written a single letter, sent any money or accepted any of his calls. He had heard they all came up and were doing good. He had been communicating with a girl name Diamond, who was around the same age and had slept with his whole clique, and she knew where they all stayed. When JC went to jail, they started using Diamond and her best friend to help them run their dope. JC had a lot to do and his job was getting in his way plus it wasn't paying enough. *Maybe I'll start playing sick for a while until they fire me, he* thought.

CHAPTER 30

JC dialed Vanessa's number while he was lying down, watching TV. It was about 4:oo p.m. He had remembered that she had told him to call after 3:oo p.m. because she worked.

"Hello."

"Hi, is Vanessa available?"

"This is she, may I ask who's calling?"

"This is JC. I met you on Facebook a couple of days ago. You were telling me that you know how to braid."

"Ohh! ok hi!" She sounded excited to hear from him.

"Are you busy right now?"

"Oh nooo, I'm just walking in the house, I just got off of work not too long ago."

"How was your day? Did you work hard?" he asked.

"I always work hard."

"That's good."

"So, what made you finally call me?"

"I thought I'd call and try to set up an appointment with you. Do you work in a shop or something?"

She laughed, "No I don't work in a shop, but I know how to braid, sweetie."

"Ok that sounds good, so when do you think you will be able to braid my hair?"

"I can do it right now if you're not doing anything."

"Seriously?"

"Yeah, I can start right now."

"Where do you live?"

"Romulus," she said.

"Me, too," he added.

Vanessa gave him directions to her apartment, and he knew exactly where she lived. They were about seven minutes away from one another.

"Hold on, Vanessa," he said clicking over to answer the other line. "Hello."

"Hey JC." It was Diamond.

"What's going on Diamond?"

"I got some info for you," she said.

"Ok. Can we meet a little later? I'm busy right now."

"Yeah, that's cool. Just give me a call."

"Ok bye." JC clicked back over to Vanessa, "Vanessa!"

"I'm still here, are you on your way?"

"Yeah, I'll be there in a minute."

Vanessa prayed to God that this stranger she was about to let in her apartment wasn't crazy. Even though she owned a registered pistol, she didn't want to use it if she didn't have too. She began slipping on something a little more comfortable.

Knock! Knock! The door sounded off.

Vanessa quickly ran to the living room, "Who is it?"

"JC."

She opened the door and he walked in, looking like he had just walked out of a fashion magazine. "Hey," he said shaking her hand then giving her a hug and a kiss on her cheek. "It smells good in here," He turned his head looking at the black leather couches.

"This is nice. You stay here all by yourself?"

"Yup, all by myself. Why, you want to move in, and help me pay some of these bills?" she joked. He laughed.

"You can have a seat. I have to get the grease and comb and all that good stuff," she said smiling, looking better in person. "You need it washed too?"

"Please," he smiled.

"Ok that's fine. Yeah, this stuff stinks," she said running her hands through his head.

"Your little dirty self."

He laughed. "Oh, you got jokes?"

CHAPTER 31

Mr Read knocked on Rita's door for about five minutes. He knew she had to be there- her car was parked right outside. *Maybe she's on vacation.* He was coming to collect his rent money for the month. He had tried to call her but got no answer.

She was never late on her rent, before, but now she was two days late. *Well, she has three more grace days, so I'll try back next week,* he thought. Mr. Read put a letter on her doorknob with a rubber band, then headed back to his car, when he saw a burgundy car driving up behind his truck.

The girl that was driving rolled down the window. "You need me to let you out?"

"Yeah, you here for Rita?"

"Yeah, that's my sister."

"Oh, ok well I'm Mr. Read, her landlord."

"Nice to meet you, is everything ok?"

"Everything's fine, I knocked but didn't get an answer. I also called, but still no one picked up."

"Yeah, I've been calling her too for the last couple days, but I got no answer. That's why I came by to check on her. I have a key, if you wanna wait a second."

"Sure, I'll wait. That's just unlike Rita to not answer her phone or the door. Even if she went out of town, she usually tells me," Mr. Read added.

"Right, right, I don't know what this girl been doing," her sister said, unlocking the door and walking in.

"Rita!" She called out but got no answer. She walked through the kitchen to the living room. Nothing looked unusual besides the burned-down candles. *She must have left these burning.* "Rita!" she yelled, knocking twice on the room door before she entered. "Rita," she pushed the door open. The room was quiet with no one in it.

Her sheets were off the bed and she could see a few blood stains on the mattress. *Her li'l nasty ass must've been having sex on her period,* she thought.

"No, she's not here. I don't know where she is, but I'mma sit and wait here for a while."

"Well, just tell her to give me a call when you talk to her."

"Ok I will."

"Can you let me out sweetheart."

"Oh yeah! I'm sorry," she said. She went outside and jumped in her car, backing up to let Mr. Read back his vehicle out, then she drove back into the driveway and went back inside to wait for her.

Vanessa walked to the back to grab all her materials. She was glad she had some type of company. All she did was work, sleep and save her money.

CHAPTER 32

"Ok so how do you want me to do it?" Vanessa asked. "Anyway, you want too. Do a design that you like," JC said.

His hair was in a big afro as she had just finished washing and blow drying it. "Are you mixed?" she asked.

"Yes, I have a quarter Cherokee in me."

"Wow! I do too," she said.

"Oh, ok."

"You can turn the TV to whatever. Here's the remote." JC clicked through until he was on the music channel.

"You gotta lot of liquor on that bar over there. You drink like that?" he joked.

She laughed, "No, I just have it here for company and

decoration. I mean, I drink a little but not how you trying to make it seem. You drink?"

"Somewhat, I'll have a drink every now and then. Why, do you want to have a couple drinks with me when we get done?"

"Sure, I'll have a couple drinks with you," she said, trying to remember that he is 21.

"What do you like to drink?" he asked.

"I like smooth drinks, mainly vodka."

"You like Goose?"

"Yeah I like Goose. Why, is that what you drink?" she asked.

"Yeah, that and Trone."

"Trone! Boy you crazy, I have Trone over there, but I don't touch it. Trone will have you out there."

They both laughed.

"So, you're not going to drink Trone with me?"

"Boy! What are you trying to do? We will be in here having sex or something! I'm not drinking Trone," she said laughing.

"Just one shot, and we can sip on the Goose. One won't do anything to you, plus, I wouldn't let you get out of line anyway. I can handle my liquor."

"I don't know yet, I'll have to think about that. I'll definitely have a drink of Goose with you though."

"Ok that's fair enough. I don't want to pressure you."

She started laughing, "You are a trip," she joked, thinking about that shot of Trone. It took her about three hours to do his whole head, because they were mostly talking and laughing. Vanessa liked her new friend as he was very easy to talk to. She hadn't laughed like that in years. This was her new secret friend and she wasn't telling a soul.

CHAPTER 33

"That's enough," Vanessa said, holding her glass as he poured vodka in it.

"What do you mix it with?"

"I put orange juice and cranberry in it. Just a little bit, though."

"Let me try that. Sounds good, I usually drink lime juice with mine."

"Oh yeah, that's good too, but this is better," she said, giving him her cup to drink from.

"Mmm, it's good. Hook me up," he said, handing his glass to her smiling.

"What do you want to do? Watch a movie or play some cards or something?"

"It doesn't matter JC. We can watch a movie."

JC went over to her DVD collection in her living room and

flipped through her movies, looking for something to watch. "What about this?" he held up a movie.

"That's fine. It's one of my favorites but hold on a second. I thought you said you would teach me how to work Facebook."

He quickly jumped up. "Oh, sure, we can do that. Where's your computer?"

"In the back room."

She walked in front of him, leading him to her room. He couldn't help but notice her curves. He entered her room and was very surprised by her cream wood and dark marble seven-piece bedroom set. Plus, she had a nice twelve-piece comforter set on her bed with about half a dozen pillows.

"Damn, Nessa, this is nice."

"Thank you."

"You welcome . . . It's ok for me to call you Nessa, right?"

"Yeah that's cool, I kind of like that." She sat in the leather chair at her computer, and JC showed her how to work Facebook.

"Is that all you want to learn?"

"Yeah that's it for right now, I'm pretty much cool on everything else, thank you."

CHAPTER 34

"I almost forgot, how much do I owe you?" he asked.

"Nothing, don't worry about it."

"No really, how much, because I'll need it done more than just this one time. I know you're not going to keep doing it for free."

"Yes, I will, I'll do it until you meet a girlfriend on Facebook that can braid."

They both laughed, "Yeah right," he said.

"You still want to watch a movie?"

"Yeah, we can do that."

"Where do you want to watch it? In here or in the living room?" she asked.

"It's cozier in here, let's stay. But first take a shot with me."

"Shot of what? Not Trone?" she laughed.

. . .

"Ok then, Goose."

"Ok."

They walked to the kitchen, each pouring a shot of Goose and drinking it.

———

Rita's sister Tai flicked through the channels for about ten minutes until she realized nothing was on. *Damn, where the hell is she?* She thought to herself, calling her again. She still didn't get an answer. She went into the kitchen and opened the refrigerator. *She stay stocked up, let me see: Reese's, pineapples, strawberries or a bagel? I'll have a bagel.* She took the bagel out along with the cream cheese and started walking around the house eating her bagel looking for something to do. She went back to Rita's room, opening the door all the way this time, seeing her sister's computer desk sitting behind the door. *Ok I'll go on the internet for a little while.* She walked in, seeing the computer in full view. *What the hell!*

She saw the holes in the computer then began looking around the room at the walls. She noticed the blood on the bed again. *That shit kind of dark,* she thought. She began shaking and getting nervous as she walked towards the closed closet door. *Please God don't let this be!* she slowly opened the closet door, seeing more blood everywhere on the floor. Her sister was wrapped in a white sheet.

Blood was all over the closet. Tai screamed at the top of her lungs, then passed out.

CHAPTER 35

Diamond arrived at Dre's house where she always met him to drop off his money. It was still early in the morning. She knocked on the door twice before Dre answered.

"Who is it!"

"Diamond!"

Dre opened the door with his gun in his hand, "Damn, you over early as hell. What's good, ma?" he said, letting her in his home. All he was wearing was a pair of boxers.

"You have company?" she asked.

"No, If I did, you would still be knocking," he joked, walking into the bathroom to brush his teeth.

She laughed, "You wrong, I do any and everything you ask, and you would play me like that? You would leave me outside just knocking?"

"Naw Diamond, chill out, you know I was just playing with your sensitive ass."

She walked into his kitchen to unlock the back door by the basement. "You have anything to drink?" she yelled.

"Nope, just water."

"Damn, I'm thirsty," she said walking through the house into the room he was in.

"I got something that will take care of that," he joked.

She laughed, "I bet you do, but I ain't bout to suck no dick this morning, I ain't in the mood."

"What you come through early for?"

"To give you your money," she said.

"Oh yeah! I forgot, did they like it?"

"Yeah, they were satisfied. They said they would call you sometime next week."

"Well how much did they give you?"

"$3,400. How much I get?" she smiled.

"How much you need?"

"Just give me a hundred."

"Bet." Dre gave her a hundred-dollar bill. He couldn't believe that's all she asked for this time. He began counting his money, making sure everything was there.

"Why don't you give me some of that dick before I leave," she said, running her hands down his chest, down to his boxers.

"That's what you want?" he asked, unbuttoning her shirt. She was almost naked, thinking where the hell is JC? She pushed Dre to the far wall, away from his gun that sat on the dresser, kissing him on his neck and lips aggressively. She was breathing hard and was hoping that JC came before they started having sex, because Dre would be pissed when he found out she was on her period. He started sliding her pants down, while kissing her. *Shit, think fast Diamond, think, think, think!* she said to herself. She quickly kneed him as hard as she could in his groin, causing him to bend over.

"Arrrrrgh, you bitch! I'mma kill you!" He grabbed her by the back of her pants as she tried to run away, but he couldn't hold her long. He was in too much pain. She broke away and ran for his gun.

"Don't move!" she yelled, pointing it at Dre.

"Bitch, what the hell you think you're doing?" he said, still in pain.

"JC! JC!" she screamed.

CHAPTER 36

J C came running to the back of the room with his gun drawn.

"What the fuck took you so long?" she yelled.

"The fucking screen door was locked, I had to come through the front door!" He looked over at Dre on the floor, then walked over to him with his gun. "Give me a reason why I shouldn't blow your head off, Dre?" He kicked him directly in his face with his foot.

"Arrrrrgh." Dre was in pain and all he could see was JC holding a gun with a silencer on it. He hadn't seen or talked to JC since he came home. He noticed that he had put on a lot of muscle.

"Get yo' bitch ass up!" JC spat.

"Chill out man, I . . . I . . . what's up man..."

"You know what's up, you fake-ass nigga," JC hit him in the head with the gun.

"Arrrrgh," Dre mumbled, spitting at JC, aiming for his face.

JC kicked him in his stomach. "You dirty muthafucka! Where the fuck is the money?"

"Man . . . man . . . I don't have nothing, man. All I got is that $3,300 on the dresser and a little money in the pocket of them jeans over there."

"He lying JC," Diamond said, still holding the gun.

JC became mad instantly and shot Dre in his leg. "Nigga, you think I'm playing with you!"

"No! No! Wait! Wait! Ok! Arrrrgh . . . . I got a safe in the basement, man! Take it, man! Take it all!"

Dre was in pain, breathing super hard. He didn't think JC would shoot him. "20, 26, 11 is the combination! Man, take it!"

JC put the $3,300 that was on the dresser in his pocket, then he took a wad of money out of Dre's pants.

"You coming with us!" JC grabbed Dre by the leg and dragged him out of the room all the way down the basement stairs. "Where is it!" JC yelled.

"Over there in the corner man, Damn!"

Dre was bleeding all over. His legs were numb, his head was spinning, and he had left a track of blood through the whole house.

JC went over to the safe. The safe opened right up. There was a half kilo of cocaine in plastic and two stacks of cash. "How much is this?"

Dre was holding his leg still in pain. "Man, JC. . . It's twenty grand, man! Fuck, man! Get me an ambulance!" he yelled.

"Fuck you! You disloyal mutha fucka! You ain't no G."

JC shot him four more times. The bullets ripped through his chest and blood leaked from his body all over the basement floor.

"You gonna leave him here?" Diamond asked. This wasn't her first time seeing a dead body and damn sure wouldn't be her last.

"Yeah, I'mma leave him here. What kind of question is that? You keep asking stupid questions I'mma leave your ass here with him."

JC's words hit her like a punch to the stomach. Then he smiled. "I'm just fucking with you, let's get out of here."

CHAPTER 37

Diamond remained silent, walking up the stairs. She knew JC probably didn't trust her, but he didn't have to worry. There was no way she was gonna tell on him, no matter what.

Diamond was a ride or die chick and JC knew that. "JC, you trust me, right?" she asked, not wanting to die next.

"Yeah, I trust you. If you do tell someone, I promise before I get to jail, I'mma put a bullet through your pussy."

Diamond swallowed hard desperately trying to put out of her mind the image of a bullet shooting up her vagina. "I swear I'm not going to say shit, JC."

"That's one down. We got four to go." he said.

JC grabbed her and pulled her close while she cried. "I believe you," he said, rubbing her back. "Come on now, we got to get the hell out of here. Put this shit in your purse."

She put the money and drugs in her purse, and they walked out the front door. They both got in the car and drove off. JC drove all the way to Welma's condo.

"Whose shit is this? This is nice," Diamond said when they pulled up.

"Stop being so nosy! Come on!"

They walked in together. Welma had already gone to work and wouldn't be back for a while. JC and Diamond put everything on the bed, unwrapped the money and counted it out. It was $20,000, just like Dre said.

"How much money you think you deserve for this job?" JC asked.

"Half," she said.

"Damn, straight up! Ok take this half key, it's probably more than that, and whatever you make off of that, it's yours."

"Ok I'll work with that," she said.

JC didn't want the cocaine. He was done with drugs. All he wanted was the money. He threw about $26,000 in his safe before he closed it. Then he grabbed his cell phone that was ringing. *Kelly.* "Hello."

"Hi JC, what are you doing?"

"Nothing, chillin. What's up with you? I've been missing you."

"Nothing. On my way to Saginaw."

"When can I see you? Let's go out or something."

"You know I don't go out, but I'll call you when I'm on my way back and we can figure something out."

"Ok that's cool, call me."

"Ok bye."

JC hung up the phone.

"Damn, who was that? You all cheesing and shit," Diamond joked.

"One of my little friends. Ain't nothing. Stop being so nosy," he joked back.

She laughed, "Whatever!"

"You ready for me to take you to your car?"

"Yeah, if you ready."

"You want some dick before you leave?"

"I'm on my period JC. Maybe next time."

"Awww, you on that bullshit, but ok."

"For real, I wouldn't lie. I love having sex with you."

"Yeah, yeah, yeah."

JC drove her back to her car. He had to drive her all the way back to Southfield. "I'll talk to you in a couple days."

"Ok bye," she said.

"Don't be running your mouth, Diamond."

"I'm not. Bye boy."

CHAPTER 38

Diamond slid in her jeep and drove off. She called her cousin Cradle right away. Cradle was a big drug dealer out of Detroit. She figured if she called him and gave him a nice price, he would buy what she had right now. His phone rang three times before he answered.

"What it do, lil cuz?"

"What you doing Cradle? You busy right now?"

"I ain't doing shit, just over here on the block for a minute."

"On Joy Road?" she asked.

"Yeah, why, what's up?"

"I'm about to come over to talk to you about something."

"How long you gonna be?"

"Ten minutes."

"Ok c'mon."

Diamond hung up the phone and headed to where Cradle was. She hated going to that side of Detroit because of all the murders and robberies. Diamond knew her cousin didn't mess around with Dre, so he wouldn't question her about where she got the cocaine from. She pulled up in front of the house, and he was standing in front along with his crew. She parked behind his orange Corvette and stepped out. She went up to him and gave him a hug. "Can we go in the house?" she whispered.

"Yeah, c'mon."

They walked inside and went through to the kitchen. Diamond set her purse down on the counter and pulled out the half kilo of cocaine and a gun.

"Damn, girl! What the hell you got going on!" He said, surprised.

"You still fuck with the powder? If so, just go ahead and cash me out for this. I'll give you a good price you can't refuse, and I'll throw this gun in for free."

He looked at her in shock. His little cousin was trying to sell him some cocaine. He laughed, unwrapping it to see how good it was. "How old are you now, Diamond?" he asked.

CHAPTER 39

"I'm 20, why?"

"I just asked."

He broke the cocaine apart, "Damn, this looks like some good dope."

"It is," she said, not really knowing if it was good or not. She just knew everybody she was delivering to for Dre liked it.

"How much it weighs?"

"Get your thing," she smiled, not able to think of what the dope boys called their scales.

"My skate? Hold on." He went to the back and brought back a nice size digital scale. He put all the cocaine on it. It read out 522 *grams*. "This is just a little bit over half a key. Diamond, how much you want for it?"

"How much you be paying?"

"Girl, I don't cop half keys. I get this shit by the busload. I'm a boss out here. How bout I give you $7,000? I usually pay like $13,500 for each key I buy."

She nodded, thinking how much more she could make if she sold it herself in balls and ounces. *Don't be greedy, this all free money,* she thought.

"Ok give me $7,000."

Cradle pulled a big wad of money out of his right pocket and started counting out $7,000 in hundred-dollar bills. "You said I can have the gun too, right?"

"Yeah, go ahead," she told him, grabbing her money off the counter. "Thank you, Cradle. I love you." She smiled from ear to ear, hugging him.

"You welcome. No problem, you hooked me up. I ain't gonna ask what you out there doing because that's your business. You a grown woman, just be careful and if you get some more shit like this, just bring it through. You ain't gotta call before you come. Somebody always here and they will cash you out right on the spot."

"Ok Cradle. I'll call you if something else comes up."

"All right."

Cradle walked her back out to her Jeep, and she drove off happy as ever. She had $7,000 in cash. She called her partner in crime. *Maybe I'll take her shopping today,* she thought dialing her number. It rang about eight times before Tai answered the phone.

"Hello," a crying voice answered.

"Tai? What's wrong?"

"My ...my ....my ...." she kept crying.

"Hi, this is a friend of the family," Maria took the phone and said.

"Is everything all right?" Diamond asked. She couldn't drive when she heard Tai crying, so she pulled over.

"No, she found her sister dead."

"Oh my God! Rita?"

"Yes, Rita was murdered."

"Oh my God. Where ya'll at?"

The lady on the line gave Diamond directions. She wrote everything down.

"Tell Tai I'm on my way right now."

"Ok sweetie, I will. Just get here soon because she's not taking it very well at all."

"Ok I'll be there," Diamond assured her.

Diamond pulled back on the road and headed to where Tai was. She was in shock, crying and trying to drive at the same time. She was just crushed by the bad news. All she could think about was Tai and how she felt. Then she thought about JC and how shocked he would be to hear what happened to his ex. *Why would someone kill Rita!* she thought to herself with tears flowing down her face.

She drove with her window wipers on, thinking it was raining just because she could barely see. She couldn't stop crying and was starting to get a headache. The thirty minute ride seemed like two hours but, she finally made it, safe and sound.

CHAPTER 40

J C hadn't heard from Diamond in about a week. Her phone was off, and he had no other way to get in touch with her besides waiting on her to call. Funerals were held for Rita and Dre. JC attended both of them, sitting in the front row each time. He had seen all of his close friends there. Diamond didn't come to Dre's funeral and neither did Tai.

All of JC's fake friends came up to him and hugged him and gave him their numbers and told him to call them. Nobody knew exactly who had murdered Dre, but they had ideas. JC never crossed their minds. Rita's murder was also unsolved. JC found out a lot of info at the funeral. He found out that Diamond was best friends with Rita's sister Tai. He hoped and prayed that people wouldn't link the murder to him.

Diamond was the only one that knew anything. He wondered if she thought he had something to do with Rita. *Naw, there will be no way Diamond will figure that out. As far as she knows, I kill for money. Rita didn't have money that was worth killing for.*

"What you want to eat this morning?" Welma asked, lying in bed right alongside him, about to get ready to go to work.

"I don't know, it doesn't matter."

"Ok I'll make some grits and eggs."

"That's fine," he said, getting aroused by Welma's soft hands rubbing his dick. She eased her head under the covers, pulled down his boxers and stuffed him in her mouth. Stroking him up and down, she sucked hard, like usual. She made sure he was at his full length before she straddled him and started riding. He lay there for a while, watching her work as he enjoyed the feeling of being inside her warm, wet pussy. She moaned as she rocked back and forth, rolling her hips and belly at the same time. She was so wet. He massaged her titties gently with one hand while he stuck his middle finger in her mouth. She sucked and licked his finger while grinding faster and moaning louder. She called out his name several times, moving her hips in a circular motion. He moved his body along with hers, feeling ready to explode soon. Welma began to shake, telling him not to stop while she rocked faster, releasing her fluids. JC came inside her seconds later, then she collapsed on top of him.

"I love you," she said, breathing hard in his ear.

"I love you, too," he lied, telling her what she wanted to hear.

"I'm going to go take a shower and get ready for work," she said. Welma got out of the bed and walked to the bathroom.

CHAPTER 41

J C stayed in bed, waiting for her to bring him a warm rag. "Here you go," she said, handing him a towel.

"Thank you," he replied, then started cleaning himself.

"You're welcome."

She went and got in the shower. JC got out of the bed and put his boxers and shorts on. When Welma got out of the shower, he was lying down watching TV. She cooked his breakfast, gave him a kiss and went to work. JC ate his grits and eggs then decided to get on the computer. He had a lot of messages. He opened the first one. It was from Jamie.

Hi stranger. How are you? Me, I'm fine, just wondering when I'm going to be able to see you again. I'm missing you so much. You just don't understand that night you made me feel so good, it was unbelievable, write me back soon. I need to feel you inside me. "Jamie"

JC took a minute and thought back to that day. Jamie had made him cum back to back, like no other woman. She was good in bed.

What's up Jamie? I'm fine, how about yourself? I'm always available, all you have to do is call when you're ready. I've been missing you too, call me later this week. "JC"

JC sent his message then clicked to the next one. It was Vanessa.

Hey JC, whatcha doin'? I miss your company, thanks for the great time. I know you will be needing your hair braided pretty soon. So just call when you are ready. Maybe I'll have that shot of Trone with you next time. LOL call me soon. "Vanessa"

JC laughed to himself and thought, *yeah, I might be able to get in her panties next time.* He went to his third new message.

Hi, my name is Kiesha, I was wondering if I can get some of that dick. "Kiesha"

JC wasn't surprised by the message as he received loads of silly messages like that. Even though the girl was dead-ass serious, she was not what he was looking for. She was all bent out of shape and she wore a lot of makeup. He did not reply back to her, but just went to the next new message.

Hi baby, I want to invite you to dinner at my house if you don't mind. Call me when you get this. "Kelly"

That was a surprise. Kelly wanted to cook for him. That meant she was feeling him. He couldn't wait to call her and get over to her house. This was the woman he wanted. This was the woman he was going to get pregnant. They both liked each other very much but didn't know much about each other. That, however, was to change very soon.

CHAPTER 42

JC didn't respond to her message either. His plan was to call her and set up a time. He was going to push for a sleepover. Hopefully she would let him. All he had to do now was think of something to tell Welma. That's where he was sleeping every night, so he had to have a good explanation for being out all night with her car. He thought about calling her, then changed his mind. He was just going to leave a letter and she could call him later and ask questions.

By then it would be too late, or he could just not answer and say he was asleep, then explain in the morning. If everything worked out like he planned, he would have Kelly wrapped around his finger by tomorrow. It was almost like she already had him. He really liked Kelly a lot. So what if she wasn't giving him money. He saw past all that. Even though she was white, he still wanted to have a family with her. This was the first white girl he ever liked this much. It was like he was hooked at the first date. Some people call it love at first sight.

He clicked back to check his next message. It was Marvin. *Is he gay or something, why he keep sending me messages?* he thought.

What's up man? I've been waiting on you to holla at me so we can hang out with some girls. I ain't no crazy person, I'm not gay and I got money. You seem like a cool dude, that's why I'm tryna hang out with you. Get back with me soon. "Marvin"

JC didn't reply. He clicked back to his home page to do some editing. He wanted to change his music. He still had that "Separated" song on there that he stole from Vanessa's page. He clicked on *edit* then went to music to look for an artist. He typed in a local rapper from Pontiac he had heard about.

JC bobbed his head to the rhythm of the beat, singing along with him. He got out of the chair and let the whole song play and repeat itself as he got in and out of the shower. He sprayed his cologne on, then took off his wave cap, revealing his well kept braids that hung to his back. Time was moving fast as he was still listening to music off the computer he had downloaded. He walked out of the room dialing Kelly's number.

"Hi, JC."

He laughed, "What up baby?"

"Nothing, just getting ready to go a few places. Did you get my message?"

"Yeah, I got it, that sounds like a good plan. What time you want to make that happen?"

"Maybe 6:00 p.m. or something."

"Ok that works, what are you cooking?"

"How does steak and potatoes sound with mac and cheese?"

"Mmm, that sounds perfect."

They both laughed.

"Ok. Well, call me later, I'mma go get everything together," she said.

"Ok talk to you later."

Kelly hung the phone up and resumed talking to one of her drivers. She was walking through the house making sure everything was normal and making sure she didn't find anything illegal.

"I've already paid the girls, and this is about $900," Ray said, handing her a white envelope. Business was great, and Kelly just stacked her money to the ceiling. She picked up money every day of the week from both houses, no matter if there was rain, sleet or snow outside. That was her job.

"Ok thank you, I'll see you tomorrow," she said, walking out of the door.

CHAPTER 43

J C phone rang, an unknown number. *Who the hell is this,* he thought, not really wanting to answer. "Hello."

"Hey JC, what you doing?"

"Nothing. Who is this?"

"This is Diamond, I'm-."

He interrupted her quick. "Where the hell you been?! What's up with your phone and shit?"

"I've been chilling with Tai. I lost my phone. I had to get another one," she said.

"Oh, ok. I thought you bailed out on me."

"Naw, never that," she said.

"Well, what's up?"

"I'm ready to handle some business."

"Who you got in mind?"

"Well, I just left Ant's house. I told him I'd be back in an hour, because he was cooking crack. The whole house was stinking!"

"Ok what's the plan?"

"Ain't nobody there but him. When I go back over there, I can have you with me. Ain't like he going to be mad. I saw him talking to you at Rita's funeral and he said he couldn't wait for you to call him."

"Oh, really?" he said.

"Yeah."

"Naw, we got to think of something better than that."

"We don't have time to think. He got a little money over there and some dope we can take right now."

"So you saying, we both go back and I just walk in and kill him?"

"Yup!"

"Wow! I got this. Meet me at the condo."

"Ok."

"How long you gonna be?" he asked.

"About thirty minutes."

"Alright."

JC grabbed his gun, sticking it in his pants and covering it with his shirt. He got off of the computer and rushed for the closet. When Diamond showed up, it looked like she had just had a makeover.

"Damn, Diamond, you looking good as hell!" JC said, closing the passenger door and leaning his seat back as far as it could go."

"Thank you," she smiled, already knowing she was breaking necks today.

"Damn, you looking REAL good, let me kiss your fine ass or something before we pull off."

She blushed and leaned over to him as he stuck his tongue in her mouth. They kissed for a while, sitting in the driveway. She tasted so good to him, he didn't want to stop. He reached over and slid his hand under her dress, moving her thong out of the way to finger her slowly. She was so wet and warm. As soon as he got deep, she started sucking his lips and moaning. He moved nice and slow inside her, french kissing her until she came.

"Oh my God! JC, why did you do that?" she said, pulling away from him.

He started laughing. "What are you mad at me for?"

"Because my seat is all wet. Hand me that shirt back there on the seat."

She cleaned herself and the seat then she started to drive away.

CHAPTER 44

"Go to the gas station real quick," he said. He got out of the car and went straight to the bathroom to wash his hands. Diamond's pussy was smelling like old, fishy garbage. The whole Jeep smelled like that. JC washed his hands several times before he left the bathroom. *Damn, that bitch stank, what the hell was I thinking? I know she had to smell that shit.* When JC walked back to the Jeep, Diamond had all of her windows down. When he got in, it smelled like she sprayed strawberry air freshener in the car.

"What did you get? You could've asked me if I wanted something."

"I ain't even got nothing. I was just tryna wash my hands. That cat was stankin' like a mutha fucka! You better take your ass to the clinic, asap. That shit was horrible."

Diamond just looked at him, surprised to hear those words come out of his mouth. "What?! Boy, please! What the fuck ever!" Now she had an attitude.

"How the fuck are you going to get mad at me, because yo' pussy stank? I'm trying to help you out. Go to the clinic and see what's up."

She didn't want to hear it anymore so she turned her radio all the way up. JC just shook his head. *Why the hell is she mad at me? Maybe I should have said it in a nicer way. That shit smelled so bad though, she lucky I ain't just smack her stankin' ass. I can't believe she's looking that damn good, but her pussy smells like garbage.* He laughed to himself.

Finally, they pulled up to Ant's house. It was pretty nice. He was only 22 years old but had come up. He had all new siding on his house and a nice ride parked out front. Diamond pulled up into his driveway right behind his car. They both got out. Diamond slammed her door hard.

"Bitch, you better stop acting fucking stupid before you end up dead in here with this nigga," he said, trying not to be too loud.

"I'm not, it's all good. I ain't tripping. I know I don't stink."

JC just shook his head. *Maybe she didn't think it smelled bad.*

Diamond knocked on the screen door and Ant opened it right away.

"What's up, my dog?" he greeted JC.

"What's good with you?"

They gave each other handshakes. Ant started walking in front of them on his way to the kitchen. You could smell the aroma of the crack. He was still cooking. Before Ant could get out of JC's sight, JC pulled out his gun and fired four times, hitting Ant by surprise in the back of his head, neck, and shoulders. Blood splashed on the wall and he fell to the floor. He died instantly. Diamond's eyes grew as big as apples after the shots.

CHAPTER 45

"Damn, that was simple, I guess you didn't have shit to say to him, did you?"

"Nope." He stepped over the dead body, shooting him in the back of the head one more time for good measure. They both went into the kitchen. The whole table was covered with crack rocks, small, big, and huge.

"Damn!" JC said, putting on his black gloves.

"That's gotta be damn near a key!" He opened the cabinet looking for baggies. He pulled out a brand-new box and started throwing all the crack inside. "Here, you do this, and I'll search the rest of the house," he said, looking at Diamond.

"Ok but hurry up!"

First, JC took money out of Ant's pocket. Then he went to search the bedroom. He pulled out dresser drawers, flipped over the mattress and tore up the closet.

"JC!" Diamond yelled.

JC ran out of the backroom. "What's up?"

"There go Jamar pulling up! He stays here, too!"

"What! Why the fuck you ain't tell me that, stupid?"

"I didn't think he was coming anytime soon. Ant told me to come back and me and him was going to fuck. He didn't say Jamar would be here."

"They was about to run a train on you." JC joked.

"What the fuck ever JC."

Jamar was getting out of his car holding a blue duffel bag. He was part of their little crew also."Two birds with one stone," JC said as he hid behind the door, waiting for Jamar to come in.

"Sit down on the couch, Diamond. Act like you sleep or something," he whispered.

Jamar walked in and the first thing he saw was a dead body on the floor. He looked at Diamond and said, "What the hell happened?" Before he could get an answer from Diamond, JC came from behind the door, punching him. Jamar was caught off guard and all he could do was cover up.

"What the fuck!" he shouted, trying to move out of the way. JC stopped punching him and pulled out his gun.

"You better not make one move," Jamar's face swelled up quickly. His lip and nose were bloody also.

"Man, what the fuck is wrong with you?"

"All ya'll some disloyal, fake ass mutha fuckas! That's what's wrong with me! Ya'll getting all this money out here and ya'll couldn't send a fucking dollar! What's up with that? You got twenty seconds to explain!"

"Man, word on the streets was that you was snitching! My momma's house got raided and she threw me out! My auntie was being followed! Why was that going on when you went to jail?"

"Because you stupid mutha fuckas was hot! I ain't never snitched on nobody and I never will."

"We all turned our backs on you because we thought you tried to give us up to the police." Jamar said.

"Tried to give ya'll up? Ain't no trying to it! I know every fucking thing! If I wanted to give ya'll up, you would've been in jail already!"

"Well, man, I'm sorry."

"Sorry? Sorry ain't gonna get all that hard time back I had to do! You disloyal mutha fuckas couldn't even get me a lawyer! I starved for months in the pen, trying to lift weights with no extra food to eat! I ain't even have money to write a letter! And ya'll out here partying and living it up off me! None of you mutha fuckas knew how to get money until I stepped up and showed you! What connect are you going through right now?"

CHAPTER 46

J amar stood there listening to JC while he preached. When JC met them, none of them knew how to even put dope in a bag.

"What connect do you go through?" he asked again, a little louder.

"Nino," Jamar mumbled.

"Nino! How the fuck you think you know Nino? I hooked you up with Nino and you gonna play me like that? You tell me, what should I do to you? Better yet, tell me where the money at and I'll let you live."

Jamar wasn't sure about that deal. He was almost a hundred percent positive that JC was going to kill him. "Tell you where what money is?"

JC laughed, then fired a shot, hitting Jamar right in his leg. "You think I'm a fucking joke, I see. Diamond, open that duffel bag."

"Arrrgghh! You muthafucka, I was about to tell you, now I ain't telling you shit! You broke . . . Bitch! Arggh." Jamar was burning in pain from the bullet.

"Well you know what Jamar? We about to have some fucking fun today, buddy," JC spat.

Diamond had pulled out ten pounds of weed out of the bag and a baggie full of money. "Bingo," she said,

"Here's some money right here," she said, holding it up. Then she pulled out two identical pistols, fully loaded.

"So you don't want to make this easier for me and less painful for you?" JC asked.

"Fuck you! You gonna kill me anyway! Fuck you!"

"Ok, ok, ok! I get it now." JC patted him down for more money.

He took a wad of bills out of each pocket. He stood Jamar up and took him to the kitchen, bumping him into every wall. He sat him down in the kitchen chair and told him not to move. Jamar wasn't trying to hear it. He started trying to wrestle, but JC was way too strong for him. The gun flew out of his hand onto the floor. JC picked him up and slammed him on his side and started kicking his damaged leg.

Jamar screamed until JC stopped. "Try that superman shit again and I'll kill you!" JC said out of breath. JC picked up his gun. "You wanna make this easy and tell me where the money is or not?"

"Fuck you!"

JC shot him again in the same leg. "Fuck you too!"

"Owww! Fuck! Fuck! Just kill me, you sorry bitch!" JC laughed at him. Jamar didn't want to suffer in pain. But JC needed some answers. He looked over at the stove and water was still boiling. It had to be super hot by now. He grabbed the pot of water and walked towards Jamar. "You wanna talk, or you wanna still play hard ball?"

Jamar was silent, not really sure what he wanted to do at this point.

"Ok" JC said, dumping some of the water out on the open wound on Jamar's leg.

"Arrgghh! Argghh! ok it's . . . it's..."

"It's where?!" JC asked, now getting irritated and dumping more water on his face.

"Arrrgghh!" Jamar's skin started sliding down his face, leaving it raw and oozing. Jamar was now screaming at the top of his lungs. Diamond couldn't watch.

"It's . . . it's . . . in the closet . . . . in . . ." He breathed hard in pain. "It's in a vent . . . Arrgghh! Man, fuck . . . A vent in the closet man!"

"What vent, which closet?" JC yelled.

"Upstairs . . . The . . . arrgghh . . . the fucking . . . closet upstairs . . . . It's a vent!!! You gotta open the vent! Take it man . . . Have the fucking money!" he cried, bleeding to death.

"Now was that hard to do?" JC asked, smiling with an empty pot in his hand. "Diamond, check the vent out upstairs."

Diamond ran upstairs trying to rush and get out of the house. JC was crazy, that was some nasty shit. A couple minutes later, she yelled, "I got it!"

"Bring it down!" JC smiled, looking at what he did to Jamar. A flop of skin from his forehead had melted down, covering one of his eyes.

Diamond had brought the money downstairs and put it in the duffel bag. She made two trips.

"Ok JC let's go," she said, out of breath.

"Ok . . ." He put three more bullets in Jamar, this time in his forehead. Jamar was now dead weight. Diamond had everything in the big duffel bag ready to go. They left, locking all the doors behind them.

CHAPTER 47

JC and Diamond rode all the way to Romulus, to the condo. Diamond was scared and nervous. *JC is really crazy,* she thought even though he acted normal most of the time. *Fuck it, as long as I stay on his good side,* she thought. *I can't risk pissing him off.*

Little did she know her time was coming soon. They arrived at the condo to see their prize. This one was pretty big, and JC wasn't sure if he would be able to hide all this from Welma, depending on what he kept. He was shocked she didn't question him about the new clothes he had been wearing. Welma's main focus was that JC did not start selling drugs again. They went inside and emptied the bag and started counting everything. They had crack, weed, guns and a lot of cash. First, they counted all the money. It took them a while, but the total came up to $67,728.

"Damn, that's what's up!" he said smiling.

"How much you think this worth," she asked, pointing to the

drugs.

"A lot! You can have it all."

"For real?"

"Yeah, take it. Do your thing."

She was happy and couldn't wait to visit her cousin Cradle. "Can you walk me out to my ride?" she asked.

"Yeah, let's go." He left all the cash out on the bed and walked her out. Time was moving fast.

JC's phone was ringing when Diamond got in the Jeep. He had left it in there. "Hello," he said, grabbing it out of Diamond's hand.

"What are you doing? I've been calling you for the last hour."

"My bad, Kelly baby. I was working on something. What time is it?"

"7:00 p.m. and dinner is cold."

"Damn, for real!" He ran back inside, waving goodbye to Diamond as she drove off happy and hot as a damn firecracker.

"Yes for real! See your messing up already. I knew you'd start playing games," Kelly said.

"No, no, I'm not. Tell me where I need to come, and I'll be there."

She gave him the directions and he knew exactly where to go. First, he needed another shower, so he rushed as fast as he could. He put a couple hundred in his pocket, put his $67,000 in the safe and ran out the door. He did every single thing he needed to do. Almost. He forgot to leave Welma a letter...

CHAPTER 48

Diamond arrived at her cousin's trap house. He was just getting ready to pull out when he heard a horn blowing. He looked in the rearview mirror to see who it was and there was Diamond. She got out of the car hauling a big duffel bag and went straight into the house. He followed behind, wondering what she had this time.

"What up doe, lil cuz?"

"Nothing, chillin. I got something for you," she said, dumping everything out on the floor.

"Damn! What you tryna do with all that?" he asked.

"Sell it to you. I'll hook you up."

"How much crack you got?" He asked, already counting the 10 pounds of weed.

"I'm not sure. We gotta weigh it."

He picked up all three bags off the floor and took it to the kitchen to weigh. "You got 23 ounces," he said. "But I don't know if it's good or not."

Good thing one of his customers was sitting right outside on the porch. "Jimmy, come here real quick," he yelled. "Try this real quick and tell me if it's good or not."

The custo put a rock in his pipe and lit it. "Whhooole," he said, squinting his eyes, "Yeaaah man, that shit is fire!"

"Look cuz, I'll give you $16,000 cash right now for everything, including the guns, too."

"Bet! That's a deal, count it out," she smiled.

He went to the back room to get a shoebox full of money. He came out and counted $16,000 for her. She knew she could have gotten more money, but she didn't want to take the risk of trying to sell all that. Plus, she had more money coming pretty soon.

JC knocked on Kelly's door. She had a nice condo. "Who is it?"

"JC!"

She let him in with a smile. She was looking pretty, as always. She had her hair done and an iced-out heart chain around her neck, with the earrings and bracelet to match. She also had some black high heels on.

"Damn, you looking good," he said, hugging her and kissing her on the lips.

"Thank you. You are too, but you are so in trouble for being late," she joked.

"Aww! Don't do me like that. I didn't do it on purpose. Something came up," he said smiling.

"Yeah, yeah, yeah. Are you ready to eat?"

"I'm starving! I don't even remember eating today."

"Ok then, have a seat and relax. Let me cater to you." She went back to the kitchen to make his plate. While he was waiting, he turned his phone off. *Damn! I forgot to leave Welma a damn letter,* he thought. He turned his phone back on and started to text her instead. She wouldn't see the message until she got off work later on.

What's up boo, I finally got an interview. They called me tonight to work, so I'll see you in the morning when I get off. Love you and sleep good. "JC"

JC turned his phone off and put it in his pocket. "What you doing in there?" He got out of his seat and went into the kitchen to see Kelly over the stove fixing a delicious meal. He stood behind her and put his dick on her booty. He begin kissing her on her neck softly.

"JC," she moaned, "Let me finish."

CHAPTER 49

"Go ahead, finish." he said, still kissing the back of her neck, rubbing against her booty. She felt comfortable with him being behind her for some reason. He made her feel safe when he was in her presence.

"C'mon, JC," she smiled.

"Ok I'll be sitting at the table." He went back and sat at the table and soon she brought both of their plates out. They ate their food slowly and sipped on some wine. When they were done, Kelly put all the dishes in the sink.

"You wanna watch a movie or something," she asked.

"Yeah, we can do that. What do you have?"

"How about something scary?"

"Ok that's fine."

She led him back to her bedroom. Her condo was nice. Everything was new, done in gold, cream and white. When he stepped into her room, he saw it was decked out with cream carpet, a big queen size bed with decorated pillows to match the comforter. Nice big fifty inch flat screen on the wall in front of the bed and more. "Wow, this is nice," he said, looking around.

"Thank you. Make yourself at home," she said.

"You're welcome. You should bring that wine bottle back here," he said, finishing his cup.

"Ok I'll go get it."

They both got comfortable. Kelly changed into a little white shirt and some shorts that said bootylicious on the back. The red shorts made her booty look twice as big. JC took his shirt off and just had on his wifebeater and his jeans. He was exposing his nicely cut muscles he had developed in prison. They both lay on the bed cuddling, sipping wine and watching the movie.

"So, tell me, what do you really do? Tell me something deep. I want to know all about you, JC," she said.

He smiled, realizing she was serious. She was ready to give him her all with the exception of sex. She was really interested in learning about him. "What you wanna know? How about whatever you ask, I'll answer, and then at the end, I'll fill in info if I left something out?"

"Ok that sounds good. What you do to get money?"

"I have a quarter Cherokee Indian in me, and I get a check for that every month, well every two weeks, and I work at a bank as a janitor."

"Ok well how can you afford a Lexus and a BMW SUV, if that's all you do?"

"Oh those are not mine, I don't even have a car."

"Whose are they?"

JC took a drink of his wine. *Damn, should I lie or tell her the truth,* he thought before he answered. "They belong to a friend of mine."

"A male or female?"

"A female," he answered.

"So are you like a pimp or something?"

"Wow! No, we just cool, I've been knowing her for a while."

"Well, what if I said I don't want you to drive her cars anymore?"

"Then how would I get around?"

"I have another vehicle that you can drive, or when we become official, I'll take you to the dealership to get anything you want."

Damn, he thought. "So, when are we going to be official?" he asked.

"Whenever you move out of that condo in Romulus with Welma Johnson."

JC's eyes grew big. "How the hell you know that?!"

"My boyfriend was murdered a while ago and he was a well-known businessman. He was set up and killed. I had been with him since I was 14 years old. He is one of only two guys I ever had sex with. I had to relocate when it happened, because I thought my life was in danger. So I now pay someone to read up on every guy I meet. Just to make sure I'm safe. The first time you and I met, he followed you to the condo. He was out there for a week, just to see how many nights you stay there. He saw Welma go to work every morning. He's not a cop or anything like that, he just does private work. I also know your criminal history and I know about your childhood and I want to help you. I asked him to look for your mom also, Tamia Cakes. I don't want you to be mad. You passed the test, I just wanted to make sure you weren't crazy or a murderer. I'm here for you and I want you to leave Welma and move in with me."

CHAPTER 50

JC sat listening in silence. *What the fuck's wrong with this bitch? I can't believe she put a spy on me!* "Damn, that's deep, Kelly," he said, trying to stomach everything she had just told him.

"Well, why did you ask me to tell you about myself?"

"I had to know if you were a liar or not. I'm sorry, I'm so sorry and because I did that I want to make it up to you tonight. I haven't had sex in about a year and I want to give myself to you. I want to give you my all. I want to share with you everything that I have. I want us to be together," she confessed.

Damn, is it the wine, or is she serious? I feel the same way, but now I don't want to tell her. I'll just play my part. This girl is the shit and I feel like I'm falling in love, too, he thought. He didn't say anything, but just sat his drink down and started kissing her. The alcohol had kicked in and they both felt as if they were floating on a cloud. She started ripping his shirt off, revealing his chest. She began kissing his neck, moving lower and lower to his hard nipples, sucking them hard enough to cause him to get an erection. His legs hung off the bed and she slid down, unbuckling his pants and pulling them all the way off of his body, along with his boxers. She kissed all around his dick and balls, caressing his thighs with her tongue, teasing him until he begged her to put him in her mouth. "Get it baby, get it!" he said.

After hearing him say that and watching his dick stand straight up, she knew he was beyond ready. She gripped him slowly and put him in her mouth. *He's huge!* she thought, trying to figure out what to do with all of that meat. She wasn't used to a dick that big. She was able to damn near swallow her ex's, but this one was going to be a problem. She did her best stroking him up and down, sucking as hard as she could. She ran her tongue from his balls all the way to the top of his dick then took him as far as she could in her mouth. JC lay back, enjoying the treatment with his eyes closed. She started stroking him with one hand and using her other hand to pull down her shorts and thong.

JC opened his eyes then pulled her up, taking off her shirt and bra. She stood in front of him while he sat on the edge of the bed and sucked her titties nice and gentle. She moaned, "That feels so good, JC."

He pulled her towards him. She put one knee on the bed, then the other. His dick was damn near touching her titties. He leaned back and pulled her to him, causing her to sit on his face. He stuck his tongue inside her and started moving it as fast as he could. He sucked and nibbled on her clit while she moaned out loud and rode his face nice and slow. He kept licking her, moving his tongue in a circular motion. She moaned louder, "Right there!" Her body started convulsing, and she began to grind hard against his face, He kept moving his tongue as he felt her clit harden like a rock. He licked faster while massaging her butt cheeks with his hands. Soon, she surprised him with a waterfall pouring on his face then she collapsed, unable to move a muscle.

He flipped her over slowly, then picked up her shirt from the floor, wiping his face while still looking at her. You could see her thick, juicy lips hanging, looking like they were inside out. He got back on the bed. She looked so weak, lying on her back. Little did he know, she wanted him so bad. Slowly he crawled on top of her, being very gentle then grabbed his dick and ran it between her pussy lips, teasing her a little. She was still wet and warm down there. She started moving towards him, trying to make him push his dick inside. "C'mon," she moaned, under her breathe "I want it."

He slowly slid his dick inside her, only putting half of himself in. She was so warm, wet, and tight, it sent chills through his body. He went deeper, pressing his body against hers as they kissed slowly. She was breathless, loving every minute of it. She gripped his back with her hands, digging her nails in as she suddenly screamed loudly. He was fucking her gently, like he was making love to her. She was loving it and started cummin' sooner than she thought. She started moaning louder as he sped his motion up, releasing and flowing inside of her with every bit of cum he had. His body jerked and shook as he tried to slow down, but Kelly wanted him to keep going because she was cummin' also. She started rotating her hips and using his body to pull herself towards him. They both moaned and groaned like two lions until she exploded. "Awwwwww!" she screamed. "That felt so good!"

JC's body was limp, but she could still feel him hard inside her. She turned him over, flipping her body on top of his and she started moving her body like a snake, nice and slow. It shocked him the way she was moving, but it felt good.

CHAPTER 51

JC snuck out of Kelly's condo quietly, leaving her in the bed asleep. It was about five in the morning, He drove all the way home thinking about how good of a night he had with Kelly. *Damn, that's my baby, I love her sneaky ass already, I think.* He pulled into the complex of Welma's condo.

"What the hell," he said, as he looked at a man coming out of Welma's place. He pulled his car to the side of the street to watch him. The guy was driving a Hummer.

Who the fuck is that? he wondered. The big, dark green Hummer lumbered down the street towards him. JC blinked his lights several times before he pulled into the middle of the street. He hopped out and waved for the guy to stop. The Hummer stopped but JC couldn't see inside. He slowly walked to the driver's side, as the window slowly lowered. *Marvin, from Facebook,* he thought. "Who the fuck is you?" JC asked, grabbing his pistol out of his pants.

"Hey man, I don't want no problems. I'm just over here visiting a friend."

"What friend?" JC asked, ready to shoot. "A lady named Welma."

"What business you got with her?"

"Man, it's just somebody I be fucking, that's it dog. Please don't shoot me."

"Somebody you be fucking?"

"Yeah man, that's it, I'm not over here causing no problems."

JC laughed. "What the fuck is your name?"

"Marvin, man. Aren't you the dude from Facebook with all the girls?"

"Yeah man," JC said, lowering his gun. *Ain't this a bitch! I'm glad he gave me a good reason to leave this bitch!* JC was shocked and confused. "So how did you meet Welma?" JC asked.

"I've been knowing that hoe for years. Why, do you know her or something?" Marvin asked.

"Naw, I don't know nobody over here, I just stay to myself," JC lied. "I thought you was somebody else. I'll write you back later on the computer and we'll hook up one day."

Marvin was relieved that he wasn't getting robbed or killed. "Ok man take it easy," Marvin said before pulling off.

This bitch! She lucky. If I wasn't leaving her, she would be getting fucked up this morning. JC jumped back in the vehicle and drove to the condo, pulling into the garage.

Welma heard the garage door opening so she went into the bedroom, jumped in the bed and pretended she was asleep.

JC came through the door silently and walked towards the bedroom. With Welma still playing sleep. JC went straight to the bathroom and jumped in the shower. After about ten minutes, the bathroom door opened and Welma walked in. "Hey baby," she smiled. "How was your day at work?"

He smiled. "I enjoyed it. It was cool."

"I'm so happy for you. I'm glad you have a job that you like now."

"Yeah, me too," he said, still washing all the soap off of his body.

"I miss you so much," she said, walking towards him, getting on her knees to give him some pleasure.

"I bet you do," he said, with a fake smile.

CHAPTER 52

She pulled his body closer to her while he was still in the shower and started sucking his dick. *This bitch is a phony, she got me fucked up. I should kill this bitch,* he thought. "Haven't you sucked enough dick last night and this morning?"

Welma looked up at him with his dick still in her mouth, not sure what she had heard.

"Haven't you sucked enough dick, I said, last night?"

"Why would you say something like that? I hate when you say stupid stuff like that! I break my back and do any and everything for you and you accuse me of sucking somebody else's dick? JC, I love you and I don't want nobody but you!" she cried.

JC shook his head at the lie she had just tried to sell him. "So why was there another man leaving this house at five o'clock this morning?"

Welma was shocked that he knew. "What?!"

"You heard me, you slick-ass, dirty bitch!" Welma sat in silence, listening to JC go off. "Marvin! Yeah, I know him, and he told me all about you and him. Go ahead and fuck with him, I'm through!" he yelled.

Welma started crying, wondering why he didn't get violent with her instead of leaving. She wondered why he would want to give up on a person that was so good to him. She knew he had no money and nowhere to go. *He'll be back. I'll let him walk away right now, but he won't leave all of this.* Little did she know he was on his way to the top. JC packed all of his things quietly while Welma cried on the bathroom floor. He ignored her. Then he dialed Kelly's number and asked her to come and get him. Her phone rang but he didn't get an answer. *Damn!* He called back to see if she would pick up. The phone rang several times.

"Hello," Kelly said with a sleepy voice.

"Baby get up. I'm out for good."

"Where are you? When did you leave?"

"This morning. I need you to come and get me from Welma's house."

"Right now?"

"Yeah."

"Ok I'm on my way." They hung up the phone and Kelly jumped out of the bed.

"Who the fuck is that?" Welma yelled. "Ain't no bitch picking you up from here!"

"Fuck you, I'm leaving. How else am I supposed to get out of here, I ain't got no car!"

"Walk, muthafucka!" she yelled.

JC didn't say anything, but just continued to pack. He put all of his clothes in suitcases and bags. His phone rang, about twenty minutes later. It was Kelly.

"Hello?"

"Do you want me to pull in front of her house?"

"No, I'll walk down to the entrance. Are you there?"

"Yes."

"Ok I'm coming." He hung up. "I'll be back in an hour to get my shit," he said to Welma.

"Give me my key!" she screamed.

"You'll get it when I come back."

"Fuck you, JC!"

"Yeah, ok" he said, walking out the door.

He walked all the way to the front of the complex where Kelly was waiting for him. "What's up?" he said, getting into the truck.

"Good morning, mister," she joked.

"Man, I have to come right back to get my stuff. She is crazy!"

"That's fine, you can use the truck."

CHAPTER 53

K elly drove all the way home. She gave JC a key to the condo and a set of keys to her truck. Then she kissed him and he drove back to Welma's condo.

"Whose truck is that?" Welma asked.

"Don't worry about it, I'm just trying to get my shit and go."

Yeah, he'll be back, I'm not worried about it, she thought to herself. "I should fuck that truck up!"

"And as soon as you do, I'll fuck you up!"

"And go back to jail," she added.

"Welma, keep talking."

"I will."

JC tried to ignore her as he carried his bags to the truck. He brought his safe and put it in the back seat. He had moved all of his little things, which didn't amount to much.

"Leave my key," she demanded.

"Gladly," he said, handing it to her. She smirked at him and turned around.

"Bastard!" she said, under her breath.

JC was out the door and back in the truck. He had left for good, not leaving anything behind. He drove back to Kelly's house and moved all of his stuff in. She already had a closet ready and a couple of drawers. JC settled in really quick. It was eight-thirty now. Kelly was tired and wanted to go back to sleep. She lay down and fell right asleep JC lay right next to her and looked up at the ceiling. *Just a few more people to get, and all of this shit will be over. I'm tired of all this crazy shit. I'm ready to live a good life and be happy. I have a good, smart, beautiful lady that loves me, and I love her too. After these last couple of jobs, I'll settle down with her, get my store up and running, and she can run her business and we can start a family.*

He thought like this for hours before going to sleep. He was in a better place now. Kelly was a good girl and she stayed to herself. She didn't have many friends and didn't want any. She was more than happy with meeting JC. She knew he didn't have much but didn't care. It wasn't about money. She had her own and knew how to manage it. When they both woke up, it was almost two in the afternoon.

"Do you want to go to the dealership today?" she asked.

"Yeah. I don't know what to get though."

"Well, what do you want?" she asked.

"I'm not sure, something like a Cadillac."

"I can get you one of those, no money down, right now."

"Seriously?"

"Let's go, I'll show you," she said.

They took a shower together or tried to. They couldn't keep their hands off of one another. They couldn't help it. Eventually, they got dressed and headed out to the Cadillac dealership.

CHAPTER 54

"Good afternoon," the saleslady said. "Can I help you with something today?"

"Yes, I would like to run my credit for a Cadillac DTS," Kelly said.

"Sure, come right over here and we can help you out."

The lady was very pleasant as she got all of Kelly's info and pulled her credit report, then came back to the booth where Kelly and JC waited. "You can pick out anything on our lot and drive away, zero down today, Ma'am!"

That sounded good to JC. "Damn, that's what's up." They all walked outside, looking at the cars on the lot.

"Are you looking for a car or a truck?"

"Car," JC answered.

"Ok what about this one? It's fully loaded."

She had suggested a dark gray DTS.

"Yeah, I like this one. This is the one I want," JC said, smiling.

"How much would this be monthly?" Kelly asked.

"I could do this for $468 a month. It's brand new and a really good car. You get great gas mileage and we offer an excellent warranty on this one, this week only. If you buy this car today, I will give you free oil changes for a whole year on both of your Cadillac vehicles."

Kelly and JC talked it over and decided this was the one he wanted.

"We'll take it," Kelly said.

"Great, follow me. We'll get you driving as soon as possible!"

JC hugged and kissed Kelly, giving her thanks her for her kindness. They were at the dealership for another hour before leaving.

"I'mma go get my hair braided and catch up with you later, boo," JC said.

"Ok see you later."

JC drove off smiling and happy he didn't have to spend a dime on his new car. After driving for nearly 30 minutes, he dialed Vanessa's number.

"Hey, you little stranger."

He laughed. "How are you doing?"

"I'm fine and you? Where have you been? I see I'm going to have to tie you up next time I see you. Don't give me a good time one minute, and not call the next," she joked. She had enjoyed his company.

He laughed again. "What are you doing right now?"

"Nothing. At home, by myself bored."

"You want some company?"

"Maybe. What I really want you're too young to give me."

"Oh, really? And why is that? I'm 21. What do you mean?"

"You're still a baby. I don't want to hurt you," she said.

"It's like that? So how old do I have to be?"

"I'm just kidding," she said, surprised by his comeback.

"Ok Vanessa."

"So when are you coming to see me?"

"I'm on my way right now, and I am right down the street."

"I don't think you want to come right now, I just stepped out of the shower and all I'm wearing is a towel."

"Damn, baby! Well, unlock the door and stay like that, let me show you what a 21-year-old can do!"

"Don't just talk shit, come show me!"

"Unlock the door," he said.

CHAPTER 55

As soon as she unlocked the door, JC came in with no shirt on and started kissing her deeply. She dropped her phone, shocked to see him. They made their way to the kitchen. With her towel dropping to the floor, he picked her up and sat her on the countertop. They didn't say anything, just went at each other like two dogs in heat.

He slipped on his condom and plunged right into her, feeling her warm, soft walls. They had sex for about twenty minutes in the kitchen before they both exploded.

"How was that?" he said smiling, pulling his pants up.

"That was good, but I'm not done with you yet. We'll finish this later," she smiled, sliding off the countertop.

He laughed. "That's cool. You think you can twist me up? I'm looking real rough right now."

She laughed. "Yeah, I'll hook you up real quick." She went and got all of her materials and came back to start on his hair. First, she had to take it down. "What you been doing lately, Mr. Busy man?"

"Nothing, just chillin really," he said, looking at her wearing a big t-shirt on with nothing under it.

"Chillin? Chillin doing what?" she asked.

"Just trying to get myself together, you know."

"Oh, ok. Well you need to start calling me a little more often."

"I will," he lied.

She took about an hour to braid his hair. She had all his braids going in crazy directions. He loved the way she braided his hair, nice-and neat and it didn't hurt. "What are you doing today?" she asked.

"I just moved, so I'll be busy getting situated."

"Oh, ok."

"How much do I owe you?" he asked.

"Nothing, boy, what did I tell you the last time?"

"I was just checking."

"You already paid me anyway," she smiled.

They both laughed. Vanessa walked towards the door when she heard a couple of knocks. She was still in a big t-shirt with nothing underneath but there was no way to tell unless you actually bent over to look underneath it.

"Who is it?"

"UPS!" the man replied. She opened the door with a smile, and her hair all over her head. A man stood there in a brown suit, holding a package.

"I have a package for Vanessa Fisher."

"That would be me," she smiled.

"Just sign right here, please."

"Ok thank you!"

"You're welcome, Ms. Fisher. Have a great day," he added before turning away.

"You too." She closed the door and set her package down on the table where JC was sitting.

"Ms. Fisher?" JC said, joking.

"Problem with my last name?" she laughed.

"No, that's just my first time hearing it. Vanessa Fisher, sounds good."

"Thank you."

"You're welcome. What's in the box?"

"Nothing, just some nice suits I ordered to wear to work. Something nice and casual, that's all."

"Ok I thought you had a bomb or something in that muthafucka," he joked.

"Boy, shut up!" she said, laughing at his comment.

CHAPTER 56

JC was driving up Telegraph Road, heading to the mall in Auburn Hills. He soon heard his phone ring over the volume of his music.

"Hello?"

You have a collect call from. "STONE," the deep voice said. *An inmate. If you wish to accept this call, press 1.*

JC pressed 1. "What's up, man?" Stone said.

JC and Stone had been locked up together. JC had dropped some money in his account a while back after he was released. "Nothing man, chillin. You been alright?"

"Yeah, I'm straight. I'm just chillin. I got your number from Merido. He told me what happened to you before you left this bitch. He wrote me a letter and told me last week. Man, I can handle that if you want me to, all you gotta do is drop me a little something in my account. I'm hurting in this bitch!"

"Yeah, take care of that for me man. I'll send you something first thing in the morning," JC said.

"Ok bet. I'm about to get on it right now, soon as we hang up," Stone assured him.

"What did the parole board say?"

"Shit man, they gonna flop a nigga man. They ain't trying to let me back out this bitch. This is my third time, you know. Basically, they saying they don't think I'm ready for the world yet, so I don't know what they gonna do."

"Damn, that's fucked up."

"I know, that's why I'm pissed off in this bitch. Man, I been knocking niggas out since you left."

JC laughed. "Man, you crazy as hell. You betta chill out in that bitch! Have somebody else do that hoe-ass shit . . . but anyway, what's up on the what up?"

"What, the visiting shit?" Stone asked.

"Yeah."

"I need you to call her and hit her off with some bread, she already said she'll bring it up here to me."

"Alright, well I'm about to get on that right now as she's always with Diamond."

"Yeah, but don't tell Diamond shit, man. That bitch talks too damn much!"

"Alright, I got you. Hit me back tomorrow or something. Take it easy," JC said.

"Ok peace!"

CHAPTER 57

JC hung up the phone then dialed Tai's number. "Hello?"

"What's up, Tai? This is JC. What's up with you?"

"Nothing, just chillin at the crib, watching TV."

"Let me come watch TV with you."

"Boy, stop! How you gonna cut into me like that when you was fucking my sister?"

"Cut into you? What's wrong with watching TV with somebody?"

"Whatever. You know what you trying to do."

"I wasn't trying to do shit. What do you think, I'm trying to fuck you or something?" JC asked.

"Yup!"

"Girl, stop. You always think somebody wants to fuck you. You not even fine like that," he challenged.

"Yeah, right! If I said you can hit it right now, you would be right over here."

"Get the fuck out of here! I would hang up . . . Are you serious, you really think I want to fuck you?"

She got silent, not wanting to believe he was telling the truth. It kind of hurt her feelings.

"Hello," he said.

"Yeah?"

"Why are you quiet?"

"Because you are an asshole. I don't understand why my sister was even fucking with you."

"Me either," he joked. "But chill with that attitude. I was just fucking with you, Tai. I just wanted you to know that I could care less about fucking you." He lied. From the first time he saw Tai, he had been wanting to fuck her.

"Whatever! What you call me for anyway?"

"To see if you will have some drinks with me." He didn't want to tell her that he talked to Stone yet. That would mess up everything. First, he was going to try to hit it and if that didn't work, he would go ahead and tell her why he was really calling. He and Stone weren't that close, so it wouldn't be like he was stabbing him in the back.

"Yeah, what are we drinking?"

"What do you want to drink?" he asked.

"Grab some vodka."

"Ok I'll be over there in a little while."

"Ok bye."

JC hung up the phone. *No mall today,* he thought. He had been wanting to hit Tai for so long and he was about to have his chance. He stopped at the liquor store, bought a fifth of vodka and headed over to Tai's house. He hadn't been to Tai's house since the first time he came with Rita, but he remembered where she stayed. He got out of the car and walked up to the door, knocking softly and ringing the doorbell.

"Who is it!"

"JC!"

She opened the door with a smile, wearing a short white shirt revealing her navel ring, with butt shorts. "Hey ."

"What up, doe." He walked in behind her, looking at her big booty. *Damn, she thick!*

They both sat down on the couch and JC put the vodka on the glass table in front of him. Tai was flicking channels on the TV.

"I thought you was watching a movie."

"I was. It went off," she lied. She had already had the shot glasses on the table, ready to drink.

"Well shit, I'll have a few drinks with you, then, I'm out. I got something to do in a minute or so."

"What the hell you got to do? Nothing! You always on the go. You need to sit down somewhere," she spat.

JC was just watching her sexy lips as she was talking. Imaging them wrapped around his dick. He laughed as he came back to reality. "Just because you don't have a life, don't try to put me in the same boat as you," he joked.

They both laughed and JC began to pour his drink and Tai poured hers. They both threw the shots back and continued talking, then poured another one.

CHAPTER 58

Stone walked away from the phone and headed for the weight pit, something he did four or five times a week. He went straight for the flat bench. He stretched a little and looked around to see who was in there before he started his workout.

"What up, Stone?" an old man said that had been down for 26 years. He kept himself in shape.

"What's up pops, you alright?"

"Yeah, I'm still kicking. What you got for me for my birthday? Today's my birthday. I turned 62 today."

"Oh you did? Man, I ain't got nothing for you besides a Happy Birthday."

They both laughed, "Yeah, I know what you mean."

Stone went over to the weight rack and grabbed two 45-pound plates and brought them back to the bench. He put the weights next to his bench then glanced around, looking for some 60-

pound dumbbells. A white guy was using one pair and a guy named Big J was using the other pair. *This bitch-ass muthafucka!* he thought to himself. He went over to where Big J was working out. Big J was benching almost 400 pounds. Stone walked up and grabbed the 60-pound dumbbells off the floor without asking Big J.

The two dozen or so inmates around all turned eyes on Stone, knowing he had just created a big problem. Big J racked his barbell with a loud clang when he saw Stone getting ready to walk away. "Hey dog!" He was breathing hard. "What you doing?!"

Stone had his back turned when he heard Big J's voice. He paused right in his tracks and turned around and punched Big J right in the nose with the 60-pound dumbbell in his hand, breaking his nose instantly. A blood-curdling cracking noise was swiftly followed by Big J screaming in agony. His hands flew to his face and he slid off the weight bench. Stone continued hitting him in his head with his left and right, still holding both dumbbells.

Left, right, left, right. Blood splattered from Big J's head, but Stone continued beating him to death. Blood was everywhere and Big J laid on the floor, gushing blood with big knots and dents all over his face. You could barely tell who he was. Stone got right up and went back to his flat bench. Using Big J's towel, he wiped the blood off himself, then continued his workout. The other inmates just looked at him like he was crazy. They went back to working out as well, leaving Big J there to die.

The old man walked back over to Stone. "Man, I covered the camera up there in that corner for you. I knew you were about to do something crazy. I seen it in your eyes when you first came in, but don't worry, ain't nobody in here seen nothing."

"Good looking out man," Stone said.

CHAPTER 59

JC and Tai were laughing their asses off, throwing back shot after shot. JC had moved in closer to her now. She had her legs on top of his and he was leaning against her, rubbing her legs.

"Stop rubbing my legs, boy."

"You got them on top of me!" he said.

"It's my couch, I was on here first. Go sit on the other couch if you don't want my foot on you."

"Shit, no problem, or matter of fact, I'm out. I got something to do, I almost forgot." He tried moving her feet but she used force trying to keep him on the couch, but he still got up.

"Give me a hug before you leave," she said, still sitting on the couch. He bent over to hug her and she pulled him down, kissing him with her tongue and her arms were wrapped tight around his neck. "Fuck me, JC!" she whispered, sucking and licking his ears, as she positioned herself on her back with him between her legs, wrapping them around him, not letting him go.

JC couldn't believe it. She was really using some strength. She kept her legs wrapped around him as she tried to take off his shirt and unbuckle his pants. He began to help her as he snatched her shirt off, then her bra. Once she saw him participate, she loosened her grip and started sliding her shorts down. All JC could see was a nicely shaved pussy. She was wearing no panties.

After she wiggled her shorts off, she grabbed him, pulling him to her again kissing him, breathing like she had just ran 20 miles.

As she was holding him close to her, kissing him with warm, wet sloppy kisses, she used her legs to slide his pants down. Once she got them down, she felt his big hard dick poking up against her and that made her hornier, so she took one arm from around his neck and grabbed his dick and pushed it inside her wet pussy.

"Awwww! shhit!" she moaned as she held on to the back of his neck and fucked him while he was on top of her. He couldn't even move because her grip was so tight. She had him just the way she wanted him and was dripping wet. She rocked back and forth on his long dick as she used the back of his neck to hold on for support. It felt good to him but he was uncomfortable, so he picked her up and stood on his feet as he bounced her up and down on his waist with his dick still inside.

She moaned out loud as she began shaking and squeezing him tight, then she came. He kept pumping then he pushed her down on the couch and he came all over her stomach. "Awww shit!" he growled, releasing every drop.

CHAPTER 60

JC woke up in his new home and in his new bed to see Kelly getting dressed in the mirror. He looked over at the clock and saw it was 10:50 a.m., "Where are you about to go, boo?"

"Pick up some money. Why? Do you want to go, sweetie?"

"No, I'm straight, how long will you be gone?"

"A few hours. Will you be here when I get back?"

"Probably. If I leave, I'll call you and let you know."

"Ok." She kissed him and left.

JC was so used to having breakfast made for him every morning. Now it was different. Kelly didn't cook every day. He would either have to make his own or go out and get something from a restaurant. He got out of the bed and made it up, then strolled to the bathroom to take a hot shower.

The water hitting his body felt so good. He thought about

WOMEN LIE MEN LIE - PART 1   159

Welma and how she had played him. Even though he was out sleeping around, it still affected him because she was so good to him. He broke down in tears, crying in the shower, thinking about the life that haunted him. He never knew his mom. She left him for dead when he was an infant. He had no real friends he could trust. He even thought about the people he murdered and wished he could bring them back. *What the hell was I thinking,* he thought, crying more. *Why am I not dead or in jail, why do I have to put up with all this bullshit out here! I just want my mom, that's all I want. A family, someone to love and care for me.* He cried on his knees, asking God for forgiveness for murdering innocent people. He especially regretted killing Rita. He did it almost for no reason. She was crazy about him and everyone knew it. "Why did I do that?" he asked himself with more tears.

He stood up, dried off and walked to the bedroom. He put on his clothes and sat on the bed. Pulling his gun out from under the bed, he looked at it for a long minute. *I'm the one who should be dead,* he thought. *I'm the bad guy,* he cried, tears dropping on his gun. He slowly cocked it back, then raised it up looking straight ahead into the mirror at himself. He cried more, knowing he deserved to be in hell for his actions. More tears fell and now he was starting to shake as his hand gripped the gun tighter with his finger on the trigger. He knew it was over. It was time to pay for his sins.

CHAPTER 61

Kelly drove all the way to Saginaw to pick up her money. She parked in front of her house and went inside. "How ya'll doing," she said to the ladies in the living room. They all looked like strippers, but they were professional entertainers. "Is Rob here?" she asked.

"We're waiting on him to come back right now," one girl said. "Today is a busy day. People have been calling making appointments all morning. Ever since you advertised us on the radio, our money has doubled."

Kelly knew this already, as her money had tripled. "Did he leave an envelope with some money in it for me?"

"Nope, he took it with him."

Kelly dialed his number from her cell phone.

"Hi, Kelly!"

"Hi, Rob, I'm at the house. How long are you going to be?"

"I'm coming around the corner right now. Hold your horse's sweetheart," he joked.

"Ok I'll be waiting."

"Ok. Bye."

She hung up the phone and had a seat between two of the girls.

"So, how is everything?"

"It's really good," Jalesa said, smiling.

"That's good, how about you," Kelly said, talking to the other girl, Amy.

"I can't really complain," Amy said smiling.

"Good, good, good! Well, I'm glad everything's working out for you guys. If you have any problems or concerns, here's my card. Just give me a call," she said, placing five business cards on the table. They already had her number, only they didn't use it.

Rob walked through the door and met Kelly in the kitchen.

"What's up, Rob?"

"What's going on," he smiled handing her a thick white envelope.

"That's $2,800 for one day of work! Business is crazy right now. If things keep going like this, we will need another driver and a couple more girls."

"Well, let me know what you think. I can hire someone new to drive or I can give you a raise."

A raise sounded much better. Kelly always kept her employees happy. She wasn't greedy at all. She paid them well and she made really good money. But it was never steady. Sometimes she might collect $200 from each house, then the next day it would be $1,000 and then the next might be $1,800. Either way it went, she always had a good week between both houses. She hardly ever went to the mall, and if she did shop, it was online. She liked buying things that everybody else didn't have.

"I'll let you know in a couple of days," Rob assured her.

"Ok I'll see you later." Kelly walked out the door, got in her truck and drove away, heading for Pontiac and then the bank.

CHAPTER 62

Chip, JC's other old friend, relaxed on his couch, sitting across from Diamond and Tai thinking how the hell were they both wearing all of this jewelry and those nice clothes with no job. He was only paying them so much. It just didn't make any sense to him how Dre, Ant and Jamar were dead, and they didn't have anything to do with it or know anything, but they were out at the mall everyday spending money. Tai even had some chrome rims on her Taurus. Something just didn't seem right. It was only a matter of time before he found out. It was only him and Greg left, and their money had increased like crazy since the murders.

Chip dialed Greg's number on his cell phone.

"What's up, my guy?"

"Man, what's good? I need you to come over here asap. Something ain't right, dog," Chip told him.

"What's the problem?"

"I can't really call it right now, that's why I need you over here."

"Alright man, I'll be there shortly. Give me like thirty minutes."

"Ok."

Chip hung up the phone and Diamond and Tai were all in his grill. They had no idea what he was talking about, but they didn't care, they were just chillin, waiting on the next sell. *Something ain't right, something just ain't right,* he thought. But he wasn't going to make a move until Greg got there.

Jamie called JC's phone several times, trying to get in touch with him, but she did not get an answer. She sent Facebook messages and kept calling. She wanted to let him know that her husband would be out of town for a couple of days. She wanted him to come by so they could have sex again. She had missed him so much and her husband just wasn't doing the job right. She waited a while to see if he would call back. She also signed onto Facebook to see if JC was online, but he wasn't. She browsed his page, looking at his pictures and reminisced about the day they spent together. She was so horny she couldn't help but call his phone back to back. Her pussy was wet just thinking about him being inside of her.

After browsing his pictures, she clicked back to his layout page. She scrolled down, looking at his comments. *What's up dog?* One of his comments said. It was from a dude that was online right now.

Maybe that's his friend, he might know where he is. She double-clicked on the picture of the dude that wrote the comment. He had a private page which meant she could not see any of his pictures or anything, but she could send him a message. That's all she wanted to do anyway. She clicked on Send Message.

Hi, my name is Jamie, I'm JC's friend, do you know where he is?

"Jamie"

No, I don't know JC but I know Marvin, he's a very nice guy, would you like to meet him. "Marvin"

She laughed at the game he was trying to run on her. *Another rookie,* she thought. She texted back, she was feeling so vulnerable right now, a rookie, nerd or anything with a big dick could have slid inside her ASAP.

Nice to meet you Marvin, how old are you? "Jamie"

I'm 25 years old, I'm old enough, don't worry baby. When can I see you in person? I know those pictures gotta be some kind of scam. You are looking way to good. "Marvin"

He hit her with some weak lines but today it was working, she read his message then laughed, as she replied back.

You can come see me right now if you want to. "Jamie"

CHAPTER 63

K elly arrived at her house in Pontiac. Walking in, she saw her brother on the couch watching TV. "Hey sis."

"Hey . . . what's wrong?" she asked.

"Nothing. Everything is good, it's just business is slow right now. Everybody that's calling is too far away. We just gave them the Saginaw number. They have to be busy as hell up there right now."

"Yeah, they are actually."

"Here's your money. There's like $4,100 in there." Rich said.

"Ok that's cool. Is everything with the girls ok?" she asked.

"Yeah, they are great. We have a nice team right now."

"You ain't fucking all of them, are you?"

He laughed, "Naw sis, not all of them."

She laughed, "Butthead."

JC snapped out of the crazy decision he was about to make. He had sat there holding the gun to his head for a few hours.

"Not right now. I can't go right now, I got some shit to take care of." He got off the bed and got dressed. He started looking inside the room, trying to find his cell phone, finally remembering he left it in the bathroom. When he got to it, he had 27 missed calls Most of them were from Jamie. He dialed her number back but got no answer.

Fuck it, she'll call back later. I already know she wants to fuck. He left getting in his brand-new Caddy and drove up to the store where his old friend Merido worked. Merido was 41 years old. They had met in prison. Even though Merido was foreign, he looked at JC like a little brother.

JC arrived at the store and went inside, when he saw Merido's Lexus parked outside.

"What's up, JC?" Merido said with his Brazilian accent.

"What's up?" JC said, giving him a handshake. "I'm almost ready man, for the store."

"Good, good, I just bought two more, so now I'm just waiting on you, man. This shit is good money, business is pretty good."

"Well give me a week and a half, I should be ready."

"Ok that sounds good, JC. I can't wait."

"How's your wife been doing lately?"

"She's fine man, thanks for asking. The kids are fine also. When are you going to settle down and have some kids of your own?"

JC laughed and leaned over the counter, "Man I'm working on it. I just found a good girl, so I'm going to try with her."

"Good, man. Settle with one, you'll be more focused on taking care of your business and getting rich. You're only 21 years old. By the time you get to be my age, you will have a dozen stores."

JC laughed.

"I'm serious man . . . have you had any luck with your mom?"

"No, not yet, but I should know something soon. I got a lot of things in process right now and I'm just patiently waiting until I hear something."

"Well, whenever you're ready, I got you man." Merido told him.

"Ok sounds good. I'll let you know real soon. I'll stop by sometime next week to come holla at you."

"Ok man be safe and take it easy out there. Watch your back."

"Ok I will. Oh! Come check out my new Cadillac I just bought."

They went outside to look at the car. It was clean and dark gray with chrome stock rims on it.

"This is nice, man!" Merido complimented.

"Thanks, man. Well I'll see you soon." They slapped hands and gave each other a hug and JC left.

CHAPTER 64

"Hello."

"Hey boo, what you doing?"

"Nothing, riding for a hot minute. Are you done doing what you had to do?"

"Yeah, I'm just leaving the bank right now on my way home." Kelly said.

"Ok you want to go out somewhere?"

"Yeah, where do you want to go?"

"I'm not sure. We can go anywhere you want. My treat," JC assured her.

"Let's go to a movie," Kelly suggested.

"That sounds good. Where do you want to meet at?"

"Meet me at the Birmingham Movie Theater."

"Oh, you don't want to ride with me?" he asked, joking.

She laughed, "No that's not it. I'm just saving gas and money by meeting you, you know?"

"Ok I'll let you slide with that one. How long will you be?"

"Twenty minutes."

"Ok I'll see ya in a minute."

JC drove to Birmingham and valet-parked his car. Kelly was right behind him. She stepped out looking like a model. As soon as they saw each other they hugged and kissed, then walked inside together holding hands. They bought their tickets, popcorn and drinks then went in and sat down. The movie theater was not crowded at all. They were the second couple in there. Maybe because it was still daylight. They had gotten there just in time because the movie was just starting. The lights went dark and JC leaned as close as possible to Kelly. He kept trying to kiss her. "I miss you boo," he whispered.

"I miss you too," she whispered back, and gave him a cold wet kiss that tasted like the cherry slush drink she had. The movie was good, but JC couldn't help himself. He started touching Kelly on her soft legs, moving his hand under her skirt.

"Baby, c'mon, not here," she said smiling, trying to eat her popcorn and watch the movie.

"Why not, ain't nobody watching," he whispered. "Let me just have a little head, you don't have to make me cum."

"JC!" she whispered. "You're always horny no matter where we're at, church or an elementary school."

"It's you that makes me horny. Don't get mad at me." He laughed quietly. He was reaching to take her panties off, and noticed she wasn't wearing any. "What . . . why the hell you ain't got no panties on? You been out all day with this short ass skirt with no panties?"

She laughed at how mad he got, "No silly, I took them off in the truck before I came in. I knew I was at least getting fingered, messing with you," she joked.

All JC could do was laugh. She had him damn near figured out. She knew he was going to try to do something in the movie theater.

"So that means you wanna give me some pussy?" he asked.

"JC, let's watch the movie."

CHAPTER 65

JC still continued to work his hand all the way up to her clit, running his fingers gently around it. He slowly slid inside her and felt her wetness. "Damn Kelly, look how wet ya are, and you talking about let's watch the movie."

"I'm always like this," she smiled.

"Come here, give me a kiss," he said, pulling her over to him.

"JC, we're going to get caught," she whispered.

"All you doing is sitting on my lap watching the movie," he joked.

She still had her popcorn in her hand when she set her big soft booty on his lap. He unzipped his pants and slipped his dick out, sliding it right inside her. She moved slowly up and down, feeling him inside her stomach. JC held her waist and bounced her faster until they both came. She moaned softly the whole time then she shook like she was having a seizure. "I love you," she said before getting off his dick back in her own seat.

"I love you, too," he said. "Let me make you cum again."

"JC, if we keep messing around, we are going to get caught, she whispered, quivering at what he had just said. She was touched that his main concern was to make her feel good, rather than himself. "We'll finish when we get home," she smiled.

"Ok I'll wait," he said.

They continued to watch the movie. It was a good movie and the way the actor played his part was amazing. He is truly one of the best actors, if not the best.

When the movie was over, they started to walk out. "You hungry?" he asked.

"Yeah, I am."

"What do you want to eat?"

They were definitely soul mates. They connected like a TV and a remote control. They were perfect for each other. They both wanted a family without verbally saying it. She knew everything about him since he was two years old, but she knew he was a good man and she wanted to help and be with him. She wanted to give him the love she knew he never had for most of his life. She had thrown up that morning and wasn't on birth control so it wouldn't be hard to believe. Before she told him, she was going to make sure she was.

CHAPTER 66

Greg pulled up in front of Chip's house. He walked inside, and saw Diamond, Tai and Chip watching TV on the couch. They were all laughing and chatting.

"Hey Greg," Diamond said.

"Hi," Tai said, smiling and waving.

"How ya'll doing? Chip, let me holla at you for a minute in the kitchen." Chip got off the love seat and walked in the kitchen,

"What's good?" Greg asked.

"Shit man, ol' girl, Tai wanna fuck, so I called you." They both laughed, slapping hands.

"Well what up, let's get it," Greg said smiling, grabbing the tequila off the counter.

"Ok but listen to this. When we done fucking these hoes, we tying them up because I think they had something to do with Ant, Dre, and Jamar's murders. I think they know more than we think and we gonna squeeze it out of them, no matter what. You with me?"

"I'm always with you." Greg wasn't smiling any more. He was pissed but he was still going to playthings cool. They both went back into the living room. Chip pulled Diamond up to sit on the couch with him on his lap. Greg sat next to Tai. He put his hands around her. "Will you take a couple shots with me?" Greg asked.

"Yeah, I'll take a few," Tai said smiling.

All four of them started drinking and it lasted at least an hour and a half, then they all ended up in Chip's master bedroom. Diamond and Tai giggled their way all the way into the room, drunk as hell. All they knew was they were drunk and about to get some dick. They both stumbled to the bed and dived on top of the soft comforter.

Greg began to strip Tai and Chip begin stripping Diamond. Greg took his clothes off while admiring Tai's fine body. Her booty was big but her waist was small. She was sexy and she looked good in the face. Brown skin, nice lips, perfect cheek bones and clear skin. Greg couldn't wait to get inside her. There was no way he was using a condom today. He pulled her legs towards him as he stood at the end of the bed with his dick ready and hard. She wrapped her legs around him, gripping his six inches and slid him inside her.

Chip and Diamond were naked on the other side of the bed. Diamond was on her knees trying to swallow Chip's whole dick. You can tell she was drunk just by the way she was giving him head. She was slobbing everywhere and using two hands to stroke him. She was going crazy on his dick, moaning, slurping and swirling her head. Chip grabbed the back of her head and pushed her down further, making her deep throat, one of her best tricks. He was covered with her saliva and loving it, but he was ready to fuck.

"Get up," he said, pulling her up. She got on the bed, wanting him to fuck her from the back. She arched her back, sticking her ass out in a perfect position. He eased behind her, jamming his wet dick inside her. She was warm and wet so he started pounding her hard right away while she moaned out, loving the feeling.

CHAPTER 67

Greg and Tai had switched positions and Tai was on top of him riding him backwards. She was holding on to his legs with both hands and bouncing up and down on his dick while he was inside of her. He lay back, enjoying seeing her booty bounce while he slapped her on each butt cheek a few times.

The room was filled with four different moans. The females were the loudest, especially Diamond. She was screaming like she was getting raped.

After Greg came inside of Tai, he was ready to switch. He looked over at Chip who was still banging Diamond and pulling her hair.

Greg snapped his fingers then pointed at Tai. Chip got the hint and pulled out of Diamond and came over to Tai. Tai bent over arching her back with her booty in the air, wondering if Chip was going to make her scream like Diamond. He entered her and went to work. Her booty was way bigger than Diamond's and her pussy smelled better, too.

When Greg got inside of Diamond, he was mad he had switched. Diamond had a weird odor going on and her pussy was loose. She was throwing her ass back as hard as she could on his dick. He didn't even have to move, he just held on to her waist. Every time she moved back and forth it was like he was getting smacked in the face with a used garbage bag. She smelled so bad, Greg couldn't believe Chip had tolerated that. Yet she made him cum quick the way she was working it but he didn't want any more of her after he came inside her.

All four of them had been fucking for a while now and the girls were stretched out on the bed sweating. Chip and Greg started putting on their clothes. "Man, Diamond was stankin!" Greg said.

"I can smell that funky shit! I thought you was musty, because she wasn't stinking when I hit," Chip said.

Greg started laughing, "Man, I ain't musty ever like that."

They both laughed.

"Man I'm bout to handcuff these bitches to the rails."

"Naw, handcuff them then tie their feet together." Chip went down into his basement to get his box of cuffs and rope. He hadn't used this stuff in a while. He came back upstairs and sat the box on the floor.

"Damn, what'd you do, rob a police station for all their cuffs?" Greg joked.

"Naw," he laughed. "You remember when I used to fuck with

that police bitch? She gave me all this shit." Chip had shackles and everything in the box.

They shackled both of the girls without waking them. Then they handcuffed both of them to the post. It was not possible for them to get off the bed unless they had keys. They were drunk and sleeping while Chip and Greg were in the living room plotting and planning.

Greg's job was to go to his house and get his pet snake and bring it back. Chip was going to sit and wait for him.

CHAPTER 68

K elly and JC walked outside of the restaurant, full from the ribs, fries and salad they just ate. "Well, I'm going home. I have some work to do for my math class," Kelly said.

"Ok. Well, I'll see you a little later then." They kissed and hugged, then JC drove away happy. While they were eating, he had discussed with Kelly his plans for the store. She was all for it and she offered to put in $150,000. JC figured that he had about $150,000 in his safe also, but he wasn't sure. If he did, that would be counting every penny he had. *I need to do this shit and get the rest of this money.* He dialed Chip's number private, but he didn't get an answer. Then he dialed Greg's number.

"Hello."

"What up, dog? This ya man, JC."

"What up my dog! What took you so long to call?"

Greg sounded excited and fake.

"I ain't wanna bother you. I figured you was busy."

"Naw, Naw, I ain't never too busy to pick up the phone."

JC laughed. "What you got up for tonight? I need a small favor."

"I ain't doing shit. Probably just go home and go to sleep," he lied. "What kind of favor you need, playboy. You know I got you?"

"Man, I need $700 from you, for about a week."

"No problem, I got that right now in my pocket. Where you at? I'll meet you somewhere, or you can drive out to my crib. I'm staying in West Bloomfield You wanna come out here?"

"Where at in West Bloomfield?" JC asked.

"Just meet me in the parking lot of the high school, you know where that is?"

"Yeah, I'll be there in 25 minutes."

"Alright, dog. I'll see you in a minute." Greg assured him. JC drove to meet Greg, another dude that played a fake role as a home boy when he was locked up. He pulled into the parking lot about thirty minutes later. Greg was sitting in a blue old-school box Chevy on some 22-inch chrome rims. JC pulled right next to him and got out of the car.

Greg was feeling funny about this situation for some reason, so he left his car running. He watched JC get out of the car. He saw a chrome gun fall on the concrete.

JC bent over quickly to pick it up. "Damn!" he said. He forgot it was on his lap.

Greg watched him bend over, then he put his car in drive and took off. All you heard was tires peeling out and burning rubber. JC looked up to see Greg driving away. "Bitch!" JC fired three shots in the back of Greg's Chevy, shattering the back window, but Greg kept driving, swerving wildly out of the parking lot. JC quickly ran back to his car and started following Greg. Greg was speeding, weaving through traffic like a Racer, but JC caught up to him quick. The police were obviously not in sight at this time because both cars were doing almost a hundred miles per hour in the dark night. Greg hit a few side streets trying to lose JC.

JC started slowing down because he didn't want to wreck. He couldn't see Greg anymore. JC kept driving around until he saw Greg smashed headfirst into a tree. Greg had gone through the windshield and was on the hood of his car. "Damn, I hope he ain't dead yet!" JC rushed out of his car. It was dark and no one had come out yet to see who had an accident. JC quickly walked up to Greg.

He was still moving but he was bleeding everywhere. "Give me yo mutha fuckin' address, or you dead!" JC yelled.

CHAPTER 69

"I'm dead anyway. I knew you killed Dre and them. Arrgghh!" Greg was in such pain, he could barely feel his legs. "So fuck you!"

"Naw, fuck you!" JC fired a shot close range right into his shoulder. "Arrgg!"

"Tell me something quick. How many bullet holes you want in you before you bleed to death? Because I'm willing to put them all over you to watch you suffer."

"Fuck you!" Greg kept saying.

JC got mad because he saw that Greg wasn't cooperating. He dragged Greg all the way to his car and thought about putting him in the trunk. *Fuck, he way too bloody. Fuck him.* JC opened fire on him right in the middle of the street, four shots straight to the face sending his brain out the back of his head. JC began searching his pockets, grabbing a wad of money, then quickly jumped in his car and sped off.

"Mutha fucka! I got something for his ass!" JC dialed Chip's number back to see if he would answer. This time he didn't call private.

"Hello."

"What up doe, this JC."

"What's up dog! What you up to?"

"Shit, chillin' out here in West Bloomfield. I had just seen Greg at the gas station. When I tried to get his attention, he had already sped off and I got caught by the light. I know he stay right out here in some apartments, but I forgot the address, he gave it to me at the funeral," JC said.

Chip laughed still a little tipsy from the alcohol. He gave JC Greg's address, not thinking shit of it.

"Alright man, good looking out. I'll call you sometime tomorrow," JC said.

"Ok stay up."

JC headed to the address and landed right at the apartment door 1126. First he knocked to see if someone was inside. No answer, so he stepped back and kicked the door as hard as he could. The door flew open and he walked in, closing it right behind him. He headed straight for the bedroom, flipping over the mattress, tearing down clothes in the closet and pulling out dresser drawers. *Bingo!* He found money at the bottom of the dresser. He grabbed the pillow off the bed, to use the pillowcase to put the money in. After he was done, he left the apartment and headed home to drop off the cash.

When he arrived at home he jumped right into bed next to Kelly and went to sleep, holding her in his arms.

CHAPTER 70

Officer Champ arrived on the scene to see Greg laying in the middle of the road. He called for backup before he jumped out of his patrol car. He noticed that Greg was dragged by someone from his car. He could tell by all the scrapes in his clothes. He checked for a pulse even though he saw all the bullet holes in his face and there was nothing. The man was dead, no doubt about it. Soon the ambulance came and took away the body.

Other officers and detectives arrived at the scene to investigate also. They towed the car, then cleared the scene and met back at the station. They were trying to link Dre, Ant, and Jamar's murders all together because of their tattoos. Still they had no idea who did what, because the person didn't leave a solid trace and there were no witnesses.

Chip waited for Greg to come back, but he never showed. Chip called his phone at least twenty times but got no answer. The girls were still shackled and cuffed to the bed. It was getting late, so Chip went to sleep. He slept until almost 10:00 a.m. the next morning. He heard the girls in the room calling his name, so he ran to the back room.

"What?"

"What you mean, what? Why the hell you got us handcuffed to the bed?" they screamed.

"Bitch, shut up before I blow your fuckin head off!" he yelled, pulling out his gun.

The girls got quiet, wondering what the hell was going on. "Bitch, I heard ya'll know something about, Ant, Dre and Jamar's murders!"

"I don't know shit!" Diamond answered first.

"Well, you gonna sit here starving until you come up with something!"

Tai couldn't understand what was happening. She looked to Diamiond.

"Girl, what's going on," she asked.

"I don't know, Tai, he is tripping."

"Naw, you tripping!" Chip said. He picked up his cell phone and tried to contact Greg, but it was going straight to his voice mail. "What the fuck! Where the hell is he at?" He stepped out of the bedroom and slammed the door.

Diamond and Tai sat still cuffed, unable to get away. On top of that, they were still naked.

CHAPTER 71

JC woke up to his cell phone ringing. Kelly had already left to make her rounds. JC picked up the phone, not all the way awake. "Hello."

"What up, dog! You was with Greg last night?" Chip asked.

"Naw . . . Naw . . ." He said trying to get awake.

"Naw, I never caught up with him, why, what's up?"

"He's not answering his phone and I was wondering if you knew where he was?" Chip said.

"Nope, I ain't got no idea," JC replied.

"Alright then. I'll holla at you later."

JC hung up the phone and lay back down, staring at the ceiling. "Kelly!" he yelled. *Where she at?* He got no answer.

He called her on her cell phone.

"Hey boo, good morning!" she said.

"What up, where you at?"

"I'm out, about to check these houses, go get that money and then I have to go meet with my private eye. He said he had good news for me regarding your mother, so I probably won't see you until 4:00 p.m."

"Ok boo sounds good. I love you."

"I love you, too. Oh yeah, I'm going to the doctor's also," she added.

"For what?"

"I might be pregnant, JC."

"Damn, for real?"

"Yeah, are you happy?"

"I will be, once you tell me you really are!" he told her.

"Aww! How sweet . . . Ok well, I'll call you later and let you know everything."

"Ok be careful."

"I will, bye, bye."

"Bye." JC hung the phone up. He was happy and wide awake.

"I might have a baby on the way, ain't that something." He ran outside in his boxers to grab the pillowcase full of money out of his trunk. He brought it in and dumped it on the bed to count it. He counted $72,000 on the nose. He opened his safe and took out all his other money and added everything up. This gave him a total of $189,000. That was more than enough, especially being that Kelly was giving him $150,000 that day. Soon after, he jumped in the shower and got dressed. After his shower, he called Diamond's cell phone. It rang about ten times and he got no answer.

He called her two more times and still got no answer. *Bitch must be sucking some dick or something.* He continued to get dressed, thinking about his unborn child and the new store he was about to own. First he had to get in touch with Diamond as her time was up. She knew way too much.

CHAPTER 72

JC left all his money on the bed and put his safe back in the closet. He went to the living room to get on the computer. It had been a while since the last time he got on. He figured he would browse for about an hour until Diamond called him, then he could go take care of Chip. Chip was the last man standing. JC had new messages, new comments, new picture comments and new friend requests. He clicked on friend requests first and had ten different people wanting to be his friend. He clicked on *Confirm all* and accepted every one of them, most of whom were females.

Today, Facebook wasn't that interesting to be on. He had so much more important stuff going on. He was just doing something to kill time. He wasn't looking for a new female to meet as he had what he was looking for all his life. He was satisfied and content with Kelly.

Finally, he scrolled back, clicking on his new comments.

What sup? (girl)

What's going on? (girl)

What up dog? (boy)

I miss you baby! (girl)

Just showing' your page some love, get at me (girl)

What's up stranger, holla at cha' girl. (girl)

And that was all. He didn't bother replying to any of them, but just ignored them and went on to check his picture comments. He had two comments, one of them for the picture he had taken sitting on the porch at Rita's house.

Hey sexy, are you single?

The other comment was for the picture where he was showing off his eight-pack.

Looking real nice and tasty.

Again, he ignored them, moving straight to his new messages. He checked his first one and it read:

Hi, I'm Tacara you're fine as hell, you need a real woman like me in your life. I can cook and whatever else you need me to do. I'm single with one kid, write back soon. "Tacara"

He didn't even know who she was he-had never seen her before. She looked ok but he had a woman and didn't want any new ones. He went on to the next message, it was from Jamie.

Hi sweetie, I noticed you called. I was busy at the time, I tried to call back, but you didn't answer. What's up with that? You been slacking, I think I'll have to find somebody else. Write back soon and let me know what your problem is. "Jamie"

That message pissed him off. He replied back instantly.

Don't write or call me no more, I have a girl and she's pregnant. I don't have time for married women. "JC"

He sent the message and moved on to the next one.

Hi sexy, my name is Lexus, what's yours?

Nothing really new so he signed off not ever checking his last three messages. He got up from the computer and lay back on the bed staring at the ceiling, thinking. About thirty minutes later he dozed off into a deep sleep.

CHAPTER 73

At about 3:30 in the afternoon, Chip came back into his bedroom. He had taken his shower and put on some new clothes for the day and Diamond and Tai were still handcuffed to the bed.

"You Bitches ready to talk yet?!" he yelled.

"I swear, I don't know anything, Chip!" Tai cried.

"Me either," Diamond cried as well.

They both were starving and had hangovers. They needed to eat. "Please, just let us eat!" Diamond said.

"Fuck that! You want to play games with me? Let the games begin!"

He opened his closet and got a black silencer out and screwed it on his gun. "Let's play," he said cocking his gun. "Who wanna go first?"

The girls sat in silence with tears streaming down their faces.

"I don't know anything," Tai wailed.

"Well, Diamond might know something... She's been spending a lot of money lately," Chip said.

That rang a bell in Tai's head. Diamond had spent more than $4,000 on her. She had bought rims and a lot of clothes. All she could do was turn her head to Diamond.

"What?" Diamond said.

"Where you get all that money from?" Tai asked.

"All what money?"

"Diamond, you just spent a little over $4,000 on me. How did you do it? Tell him, please!" she cried.

"Yeah, bitch, spit it out!" Chip added.

"Fuck you, Chip! I don't know anything!" Diamond said.

"Naw bitch, fuck you!" He said, pointing his gun at Tai, shooting her in her leg.

"Owww!" she cried, screaming because of all the pain. "Please! Please!" she begged. "Tell him bitch!" she screamed and spit at Diamond.

Diamond was shaken by the sight of all the blood. "Oh my God!" she cried, "Ok, ok, I'll tell you who did it!"

"Who then, bitch?" Chip said, hitting her in the mouth with the gun, causing her to spit out blood. "Speak, bitch!" he yelled.

"It was JC. He killed all of them."

"And what part did you play?" Chip asked.

"I just called them up."

"So, you set them up?" he asked.

Diamond became silent. Tai couldn't believe her ears, after all the crying she had seen Diamond do. Diamond didn't even let her in on what was going on. Some best friend.

"You set them up, didn't you?!" he yelled.

She shook her head no.

"Bitch! You lying!" he hit her in the head with the gun. "Call JC right now and get his bitch ass over here. Tell him I got $200,000 waiting for him. Tell him it's an easy lick."

Diamond cried out just thinking about what he had just said. He wanted her to set JC up so he could kill him. "You're still gonna kill me, no matter what?" she said.

"No, I'll let you go, if you give me JC."

"You promise?"

"Bitch, you gonna do it or not?" If not, you're dead and Tai's dead too."

"Ok I'll do it. My cell phone is in the living room inside my purse."

"First get yourself together. Make sure you sound normal," Chip told her.

"Ok."

He brought her cell phone to her and she saw she had seven missed calls. All from JC, Chip dialed his number back, putting him on speakerphone and holding it up to Diamond's bleeding mouth. The phone rang about six times before he answered.

"Hello?"

"Hey JC."

"What's up, Diamond?"

"You already know," Diamond said in code.

"Oh yeah!"

"Yeah, I'm at Chip's house right now. He just left and should be back in about 45 minutes. Can you get over here, right now? We can't wait until he comes back."

"Where you at? What city?" JC asked.

She gave him directions and sounded perfectly normal. All JC could see was dollar signs. His plan was to kill her and Chip.

He got his gun and rushed out of the house. He drove to the address she gave him. It took him about 45 minutes. When he pulled up, he saw Diamond's Jeep and Tai's Taurus outside, *Damn, I'll have to kill all these mutha fuckas,* he thought. Soon as he pulled up, he called.

"Hello," Diamond answered.

"I'm outside."

"Come in through the side door, don't park in the driveway, park down the street. The door will be unlocked." she said.

"Ok, give me a second."

CHAPTER 74

He drove and found a place to park, then he walked up to the house. His cell phone was ringing. It was Kelly. "Not now Kelly, not now." He ignored it, but she kept calling. By the time he got up to the door, she had called him eight times. He didn't answer and she finally stopped. His gun was in his pants and his phone was in his hand. His phone went off again as he was opening the door. It was a text message from Kelly. He ignored it, putting his phone in his pocket and pulling his gun out. He opened the door slowly and walked inside. "Diamond!" he yelled.

"Come in!" she yelled from the back room.

Tucking his gun in his front pants, he closed the door. He walked through the kitchen and Chip was waiting for him. Chip jumped out and smacked him right in the face with the gun. It caused JC to fall right on his ass on the kitchen floor, holding his eyes. He felt a bullet pierce his leg. "Aww! Arghh," he yelled, gripping his leg. Chip snatched the gun out of his pants and threw it behind him.

"Hey, buddy, I see you like playing games," Chip said laughing.

"Fuck you, nigga! You're lucky you caught me off guard."

Chip laughed. "Or what?!" He hit him in the head again with the gun. JC couldn't see anything because of all the blood leaking from his face. "So, you were coming to kill me?" Chip asked.

"You damn right!"

Chip shot him in his arm. The bullet only swiped the side of his arm, but still left it gushing blood all over the kitchen floor. Chip took out some cuffs and shackles. He shackled JC's legs together, then handcuffed his hands in front of him. Then he patted him down to see if he had any more weapons on him, but he was clean. Chip lifted him up and brought him in the bedroom with Diamond and Tai.

"I'm so sorry, JC! He was going to kill us," Diamond cried.

"Fuck you, bitch," JC said as Chip threw him on the bed then quickly left the room and closed the door. None of the three had any idea what Chip was planning. He came right back in less than a minute, with the gun JC arrived with. He saw Diamond playing with a cell phone, trying to call 911.

She had gotten JC's cell phone out his pocket. "Bitch, is you stupid?" Chip took the cell phone from her and shot her in the head. Blood splashed all over the headboard and the back wall. He took the cell phone, noticing JC had an unread text message. "Kelly says," he went through the phone trying to open the message. "After this you die, for being disloyal." He shot Tai twice in the chest.

JC knew he had fucked up. He should've already killed

Diamond. She had turned on him and now he was paying for it with his life. So many things ran through his head. He had flashbacks of every murder he had committed in his whole life. He felt sick to his stomach, but he wasn't prepared to accept death that day. Chip read the message out loud Kelly had texted.

"Hi baby, you must be busy. Do you, but I have good news. You are going to be a daddy and I'm having twins! I'm so happy and I talked to my spy. He found your mom, Tamia Cakes, but she changed her name to Vanessa Fisher. She lives in Romulus and works in Dearborn. Call me when you can and I'll tell you more, Love Kelly"

After Chip read the message to him JC heard two gunshots go off. The bullets pierced Chip's back and exited of his chest. "Arghh!" he growled, falling to the ground, dropping his gun. "Kelly?" JC said as he looked up and couldn't believe his eyes. She was standing there still holding a gun, with a crazy look on her face.

"Kelly baby, what are you doing here?" JC asked, still in pain but happy she saved his life. "We got to get out of here! Quick, uncuff me!" He was anxious to leave because he was sure that someone heard Kelly's gun go off. Kelly didn't say anything, as she simultaneously let off two more shots that went right through JC's body.

She dropped her gun, took off her black glove and walked out of the house to the Cadillac she had just purchased for JC. Her baby daddy Marvin was right outside, waiting in his Hummer alone with their two little girls...

ALSO BY A. ROY MILLIGAN

Women Lie Men Lie part 2

Women Lie Men Lie part 3

Stack Before Your Splurge

Please leave a review of how you feel about the book.

https://www.amazon.com/A-Roy-Milligan/e/B009YEVZPC?ref=
sr_ntt_srch_lnk_2&qid=1587560927&sr=8-2

CPSIA information can be obtained
at www.ICGtesting.com
Printed in the USA
LVHW081939081120
671086LV00010B/766